LOSTUNS
FOUND

by

SHARON SKINNER

Brick Cave Media
brickcavebooks.com

Cover Illustration by Keith Decesare
kadcreations.com

Brick Cave Media
brickcavebooks.com

For Windy,
Lover of life, laughter, and children.

LOSTUNS
FOUND

by

SHARON SKINNER

Brick Cave Media
brickcavebooks.com

Chapter One
Empty Nest

"Oy, get up."

Gage woke to a hard kick to his backside. He sat up, fuzzy-brained and bleary-eyed, darting looks around the dim bolt-hole. "Where is ever'one?"

"Out. Where you oughta be." Checks hauled back to give him another kick, but Gage managed to roll aside, so the blow only grazed his ribs.

The high-pitched blast of the second shift whistle made him jump up with a start. *Ding-dangit!* He'd slept longer than he'd planned. He'd come back to the hidey later than usual, his pockets still light and, even though he'd smushed into the familiar huddle of bodies, sleep had been a rotten teaser.

And now Checks was bruising him with his filthy bunions.

"Empty *Nest* time." Checks pulled back his leg for another kick.

Gage dodged the blow and dug around under the pile of rags for his worn-out boots.

The attic space above the noisy gear factory seemed more like a fort than a nest to him, but Checks had chosen the name, and no one, including Gage, was prepared to stand up to him. Especially not over something as piddling as naming a bolt-hole. After all, he was their pack leader, as well as the eldest and biggest of them.

Not to mention the meanest.

"Didn't 'spect to see you so late," Gage said, flopping down to pull on his boots.

"I bet you didn't. Notherwise, you'd like as not been lazin' about still." Checks's face twisted up in an ugly half-smile and he balled up his fists. "And I'm as taking a Boss's day off. You got somethin' to say 'bout it?"

"Naw, naw." Gage scrambled to his feet. "Just surprised, 'at's all." He tucked his ragged shirt into his trousers and yanked his gear-bag off its crooked nail. He pulled the flap open and peered in at his cracked goggles and rusty breather.

"What's wrong?" Checks tilted his head. "Think I'd rob ya in yer sleep?"

"Naw, Checks. 'Course not. Just doing a looksee. Numberizing what I got."

"What you got is a nice cozy place to sleep, and mates what depend on one another to provide. And you hain't been pulling your weight."

Gage tried not to look guilty, but he could tell Checks knew. Knew he'd been out searching. Again.

"I told you to let 'em go." Checks ground the words between clenched teeth. "They're gone. And that's the end of it."

But it wasn't. Not for Gage.

Before now, the last time a pack member had disappeared, it had been Strikey's sister, Ash. She'd gone out one evening last spring and never returned. Strikey insisted she'd met some rich merchant—like

2

she'd always nattered on about—and run off with him. He told anyone who would listen that she'd return for him once she'd got settled in right and proper.

Checks rolled his eyes every time the subject came up. Even Gage had his doubts, but he'd never be the one to crush Strikey's hopes by saying so. After all, he knew what it was like to lose someone and try to hold onto hope for their return. Leastways, Strikey hadn't run off and left Ash to be nabbed by the coppers. His chest tightened and he pinched himself to force the bad memories to scuttle off back where they belonged.

At any rate, the gang had all been careful to check in regular-like ever since. Now, three Lostuns had up and vanished in a matter of weeks. First Fingers, then Shims. And now Axel.

Checks had only shrugged, saying it was a relief to have fewer bellies to feed. But Gage didn't believe they'd all just up and decided to scarper off without a word. Something was up and he was bent on discovering what.

Checks gave him a hard look. "Well, what are you waiting on? Get out there and bring back something better than the nothing you brung in last night. Lessen you want to go hungry. Again."

Gage slung his bag over his shoulder and clambered up the ladder that led to the roof. The rest of the gang had already squirreled out into the streets. Slim pickings would be all that was left, and Checks wouldn't keep settling for less than a full share from Gage. Not to mention, Tinker was expecting to settle up, so Gage needed to get his mitts on something of worth before the end of day. No way would the old haggler grant another 'lowance. And no one wanted to be on the wrong side of Tinker when he didn't get his due.

He reached the top rung and released the locking mechanism, shoved open the wooden hatch, and peered out into the gloomy afternoon. Even with the midday sun above, the air hung murky and brown over the city, filled with the exhaust of the factories that spewed day and night.

Only when an easterly breeze blew in from the coast did enough of the wood and coal fumes blow away inland to allow the sun's rays to pierce through. Today, the air sat still and thick like a ragged blanket. So much coal and wood burned day and night, Gage thought there ought to be a better way. But, as Checks would say, "Steam don't make itself, and machines got to have steam."

He pulled in a lungful of air, testing the weight of it. When he huffed out, his throat didn't burn any more 'en usual. So, at least it weren't a full-on coughing day, and his breather could keep, which meant it might last him a bit longer.

He peeped his head out to make sure the coast was clear—though no place was truly safe in the city, especially for a lone orphan—then he heaved his gear bag onto the soot-covered roof and climbed out of the safety of the gang's hideaway.

Gage shivered, despite the warmth of the day that clung to the roof tiles. Reaching into his bag, he pulled out his dingy goggles and slipped them over his head and let them dangle around his neck. The crack in the lecture lens was still visible, though Tinker had repaired it in trade for some of the better gadgets Gage had managed to collect on his forays.

He glanced back at the open hatch of the gang's Nest. Though the space between the floorboards and the roof was only about five foot, the attic stretched out nearly halfway across the entire building. Gage suspected it had been originally built as hidden storage for smuggling goods. But it hadn't been used in ages and the Lostuns had taken up residence years ago, even before Gage had become one of them, and well before he'd become second in command. A position Checks was sure to remind him could be as easily taken from him. Not that it meant much, 'cept that if anything happened to Checks, it would be up to Gage to make sure the gang took revenge. But to Gage, it meant he might finally be able to make up for the past by doing what he could to keep his mates safe. Lot of rusted good he'd done of late.

They'd shored up the flooring over the years, to dampen any sound they might make. Being caught traips-passing would send them all to the labor house. Not that the factory ever fell quiet enough that anyone in the workspace below would hear a small noise from above. All the same, the gang had learned to be as silent as smoke inside the space.

He closed the hatch without a sound and replaced the leftover scraps and junk to cover it from any sneaky-peaking eyes. Then, he slipped on the tattered facemask that served to filter out the worst of the thick smoggy air, saving his breather for the worst times. Lately, the streets had got meaner and leaner, so there wasn't much coming in, which meant he had nothing much to trade for repairs or supplies. Except for his meager stash, and he'd need most of that to pay Tinker.

It was true. Gage had been focused on finding out what was happening to their mates. Loyalty was the gang's number one rule and it hadn't been broken in years. Now...too many members had disappeared for it to be a fluke. So, either a rival gang had moved in and offered them a brighter payday—not likely, not with the motley crew of castoffs they were—or something foul was afoot. And none of his gang deserved that. Despite Checks's warning, Gage would do everything he could to find them.

He crouched low as he crossed the rooftop, keeping away from the edge where he might be seen from below. It wouldn't do to attract attention to the gang's hideaway. Checks would be less than pleased. And when Checks was displeased, well, it wasn't worth anyone's hide doing something to cause that. Bad enough Gage was defying his pack lead. If he did something as stupid as spoil their best bolt-hole, Checks would do him up right good.

At the far corner of the rooftop, he paused and glanced back at the trap door before shifting some old rusted fittings and lifting the broken bit of pipe that held his store of saved up goods. Most of it was bits and bobs he'd hefted from around, all except the watch and fob. His empty guts twisted in a rigger's knot as he unhooked the chain from the watch. He tucked the watch back into the pipe and moved everything back so it looked undisturbed. Then, he opened his fingers and dropped the glittering fob into his sack with the rest of his store and slipped back across the rooftop. It would be a shame to give it up, but what he owed Tinker he couldn't scavenge in a month, much less the few hours left in the day.

Gage flattened himself onto his belly as he neared the pipework that wound its way up the factory's north wall before jutting up above the rooftop. The buildings here were tucked up close, with barely a boy's length between the outer walls. It made for tightly packed quarters and narrow alleys, but it also allowed the sprightliest of the gang members to leap across the space to the nearby buildings or clamber down betwixt them without being seen, most times.

Gage crawled forward on his stomach till he could peer over the edge of the factory's rooftop. Once assured there was no one in the alley, he shimmied over the side and, quick as a cat, slid down the pipe works, hissing as the heat of the steam that powered the factory's machinery scorched his hands through the thin rags wrapped around his palms.

He reached the spot where the pipes turned toward the front of the building where they connected with the great ports that belched steam up from the underground tunnels that rambled beneath the city. He stood on the largest of the horizontal pipes, preparing to make the long leap down to the pavement, when a noise startled him and his balance wavered. He grabbed at the line beside him, sucking in his breath at the searing pain. He leaned back against the factory's wall to keep from falling and tried to blend into the soot-covered brick.

"Pssst," a voice called up. "It's only me."

"By Cutter's bloody badge, Nobs," Gage grumbled as he jumped down onto a pile of rags kept heaped against the building to muffle the sound of feet landing on the cobblestones. "You nearly got me bashing my head to the ground."

"Sorry." Nobs wiped his nose on his sleeve. "Wasn't trying to cause no hurts."

"'Course not. But what're you doing down here?" Gage glanced toward the street end of the alley. "You know there's no way up from here during daylight."

"I knows." Nobs squatted next to a rusted waste bin and sniffed. "But I gots some grub for shares, if you've got the hungries. Knowed you'd come in late." He stretched out his arm, offering Gage a small hunk of what looked to be stale bread. "There's some cheeses inside it. Bit moldy, but still edible-like."

Gage eyed the food hungrily. "You ate your bit already?" he asked. Nobs was far too generous with his takes.

Nobs nodded vigorously. "Sure."

"All right, then. Tear me off a bit, but then we have to be bustling." It wouldn't pay for two scrabbly boys to be seen lurking in an alleyway, 'specially not

7

so close to the Nest.

Nobs broke the food into two pieces and handed the larger bit to Gage, who gnawed at the edge of the hard crust, attempting to work a bite loose without breaking his teeth.

Nobs tucked the remaining hunk into the pocket of his baggy pants, which only stayed up with the help of the bit o' braided twine tied about them. The younger boy was so tall and thin, it was impossible to find clothes that fit. Even the hand-me-downs from the older Lostuns were always too short and wide to fit his skeletal frame.

"Where you—"

His question was cut off by a shout and the high twee of a copper's whistle. "Oy, you grabblers! What you doing there?"

"Scuttle!" Gage shouted, hefting his sack and dropping the precious morsel of food in the process.

Nobs loped off, his long legs hauling him down to the end of the alley and out of sight before Gage could round the corner.

"Hold up there!" Behind Gage, the clobber of Constable Cutter's thick-soled boots pounded against the pavement.

If Cutter caught him, he'd surely be pigeoned-up in the local workhouse, likely chained up on a detail after his last escape, and no one Gage had ever heard of had made it out of the workhouses whole once they'd been chained. He put on a burst of speed, skittering into an alley, hoping Nobs had gotten a distance away or managed to hidey-hole up somewhere where old Cutter wouldn't find him.

But Gage couldn't worry about that now. Not with Cutter huffing and puffing behind him, determined not to let his prey escape. All the streeters knew old Cutter made two farthings for every boy he turned into the workhouse. It wasn't legal to take money for catches, but then again, not much of what Cutter did was legal, the old pirate. Nor did anyone in a position to do anything about it seem to care.

Gage ran out of the alley and across a narrow street, dodging a dark carriage pulled by matching horses. The horses startled, but the driver was skilled enough to get them under control before Gage had even shirt-tailed out of sight. Normally, he would have stopped to admire the animals, and possibly prig the owner for a half-pence, but right now his life was on the scales. He barely grinned as he heard the clatter and scuffle of Constable Cutter running smack-dobbed into the side of the carriage. The confusion gave Gage the time he needed to scarper up over a wall and shimmy himself into a narrow opening between two buildings.

He kept running even as the space tightened. Pipes and planks jutting out of the walls blocked the way through. He'd stupidly dodged into a dead end. There was no choice now, but to stick it out where he was. He wedged himself back as far as he could go and lowered himself onto his belly to wait.

He covered his head with the dark cloth of his loot sack and slowed his panting to a low hush, hoping that even if old Cutter managed to follow his escape route and peer between the crumbling buildings, he'd see nothing but a pile of rags.

Minutes crawled by as he lay in the shadows, and Gage's thoughts strayed to the missing Lostuns. If Cutter had scooped them up, someone would have seen them on a work gang and word of their whereabouts would have gotten back to the pack. But there'd been not a whisper. Not a trace, nor a hair of them. If they hadn't been sworn members of the Lostuns, no one might even know they existed, much less that they were missing. But Gage knew. They were his friends—no, they were his family, the only family he had since...Nawp, he told himself, best not to think on that. Anyways, despite Checks's orders against seeking out answers and risk drawing undue attention to the gang, Gage aimed to discover where they'd gone. No matter the cost.

***

It felt as if he'd lain there forever, yet Gage dared not move too soon. Cutter wasn't known for his patience in most things, but he had a reputation for not giving up on his prey. Once he'd seen a street urchin, he would do everything possible to nab him. Or her. He'd proven that on more than one occasion.

Gage hoped Nobs had got away. That he hadn't got hisself caught. Or hurt. A picture flashed in Gage's head. A memory he'd tried hard not to think about. A day when the Lostuns had clashed with the Dartlings. Gage felt his lip curl at the thought of the Dartlings gang. How he hated them. Especially their leader, Wynd. Even now, thinking about her made the scar on his left cheek burn. Though, the gash she'd given him had been healed for months. The rumble had been in full swing when Gage had arrived, having nearly stumbled up on Cutter and needing to take the long way round. A full-on battle that should have been fists only, had the Dartlings bothered to follow any kind of rules. But they were beyond brawlers, carrying sticks and broken bottles into the fray.

The Lostuns hadn't stood a chance against such bloody tactics and had had to fall back, losing an entire section of their turf to that bunch of scabby brats. Gage had tried to pull Wynd off Nobs, who was never able to do any real damage in a scuffle, held back by his too thin frame and his too soft heart. He could still see the glint of glass in her raised hand...

Gage stiffened. Hob-nailed boots clicked on the greasy cobbles, then passed by. After a bit, he let himself breathe normally. Dusky shadows settled, and he silently cursed himself for having left the gang's safe space when he had. Not that he'd had a choice. But it had gained him nothing. Nothing but a face full of dirt and a pant leg full of whatever bugs had begun crawling on him as he lay in the dank space.

At least there'd been no more sign of Cutter. Likely the rotten copper was even now making his evening tavern rounds, throwing down the free drinks he forced the landlords to give him in order to leave off troubling their patrons.

He rose up slowly, smacking at the insects that had crawled inside his breeches. Too late, he realized his mistake. The boots that had passed by earlier stomped back and a dark shadow fell across the opening to his hidey.

"There ya are." Cutter's satisfied voice sent a chill scuttering up Gage's back. "Now, why'nt you just come on out like a good little pup. Make things easy on both of us, eh?" The copper twirled his wicked headknocker.

Gage backed in as far as he could, to a spot well out of reach of the copper's thick knobby club. He searched for an escape, but his gut tightened. He was trapped. Cornered like a mouse. A soon-to-be-dead mouse.

Memories of the workhouse battered him, and his body tingled with the need to flee. He couldn't fight. He was no match for Cutter and his club, especially closed in like this. Cutter knew it, too. He could sense the big man's ugly grin widening in the shadows.

The copper wouldn't want to use his whistle. That'd bring undue attention. And he'd have to turn Gage over to the orphan handlers. That would probably only delay Gage's trip to the workhouse, but it would cost Cutter his coinage, and the crooked copper wouldn't like that.

Then again, at least with the orphan handlers, Gage might have a chance at escape. He opened his mouth to shout, prepared to cause as much of a ruckus as possible. If the last thing he managed to do as a free person was deny Cutter a few farthings, it would be worth it.

Before he could make a sound, Cutter let out a yelp and swung away from Gage's hidey with a curse. "Why you little mongrel," he growled, his hands rubbing at the back of his head. "I'll have your guts out for that."

Gage groaned. Nobs must have rounded back and seen that Cutter had him cornered. "Run!" Gage shouted. "It hain't worth gettin' caught for me."

"Hah!" Nobs's high-pitched laugh was followed by the sound of another rock clouting the big copper, who stood between Gage and freedom.

Cutter let out a howl of rage, glanced back at Gage, then rushed off at a run, his heavy footsteps fading away.

In a pinch, Gage burst out of the nook and headed after them, pulling up short when he saw Nobs quickly outdistance Cutter, running faster than Gage thought the younger boy was capable, even with his extra height.

Best to take the dodge while he could. Gage turned and dashed away.

Chapter Two
Losers Weepers

"I told ya ta git out of our hidey." Buller's face twisted itself into a fleshy snarl.

Wynd stood her ground. That look had won him his name, his position as the Dartlings' pack second, and had once been one of their best weapons against encroaching streeters. Many a rumble had been avoided due to Buller's ugly mug. Meaning her mates had been saved many a bloodied nose and broken lip.

Or worse.

It had once been her favorite thing about him. The only thing, she reminded herself, since he actually had no other qualities to list. "As I recall," she said, "this particular hidey was found by none other than myself. Mine by rights of finders keepers." She pressed herself against the back wall of the cramped space, her eyes darting to check over Buller's shoulder, in case any other members of her ex-gang were waiting to give her another what for. Her ribs were still bruised from the pummeling they'd given her last week during her official relief of duty and turn out. That's a laugh, she thought. Nothing relieving about being beaten on the way out by the very mates who once looked up to you.

"That was when you was still one of us. Dartlings' own what's on Dartlings' turf." Buller's face turned red, but an ugly smile crawled across his lips. "But you hain't a Dartling anymore."

He was right, of course. Though she'd hoped he wouldn't call her bluff. Or that he'd at least have let her be just this once. But why would he? He probably thought she was rethinking her decision to step down as the Dartlings' pack leader. Not that she could. No. She'd made the choice. Her brothers over the pack. Not that there had been much of a choice. Family was everything. But Buller wouldn't understand that.

Most Dartlings would likely only turn away from her, shunning her as a deserter. But there were a few, like Buller, who had chafed at her leadership enough to want to take it out on the girl who'd once bested them, just to make a point. Not to mention he still blamed her for the loss of their warmest and best bolt-hole. It hadn't been her fault. Someone had nickered on them. But she'd been in charge when it happened, which made her responsible. And, now that he had assumed the number one spot, Buller had everything to lose if she decided to try and worm her way back into their pack.

Wynd sighed and stuck her hand inside her jacket pocket, wrapping her fingers around the stick she'd sharpened by scrubbing it along the coarse brick walls till the end was as dangerous as the knife she'd given up. Along with everything else except her ragged filter mask. There would be no reasoning with Buller. He was determined to prove his new position.

And since he hadn't had to earn it through normal means, he'd want to use this as an example that he deserved it.

She bent her knees and slid down the wall a few inches, to make him think she'd given up, and got ready to run.

Chapter Three
Settling Up

Gage shifted his sack on his shoulder and headed for Shanty Town. It was on toward evening now and his load was still light. After having to run from Cutter, he'd had to scrounge in the narrow alleyways and stay away from his usual haunts. That meant no bumpty-bumps, nor pocket-picking. Just as well. He hated taking from hard-working sods. Though, most of the stingy sour-puss men he took from would only spend their extra farthings on drink, any rate. Sadly, that left only scrounging in bins and muck, which was less than rewarding on a good day, and today... today had not been good.

He skirted the area around the ship docks, giving a wide berth to that section of the city. Wouldn't pay to run into any of the Dockers. Wouldn't do to get caught by one of the older boys who ran with that rough and tumble gang, neither. They weren't known for their gentle handling of outsiders. Nor for their brains, Gage thought. But that wasn't something anyone who wanted to keep his knee bones intact would say aloud where one of the Dockers might hear.

He kept his head down, but his eyes darted back and forth as he scanned his surround. Caution and alertness when outside. Checks had hammered these things into every one of them. So, how was it that three of their number had got caught unawares in the same number of weeks? Not possible. And yet they were gone. All three.

Gage turned up a crooked side street that zigged and zagged like it'd been built by a drunken sailor. The narrow lane twisted back and forth. Rickety houses clung to either side, leaning so far over the crumbling street they looked like they were sharing dark secrets. This place sure as certain suited Tinker.

A few more turns brought him to a ramshackle cottage squished between two grim lodgers that rose above it on either side. The low-slung cottage had a narrow porch with three rickety steps leading up to it. Gage made sure no one was out on the street before he approached Tinker's stoop. Skipping the broken second step, he hopped up onto the porch, rapped three times on the wooden door, waited two breaths, then rapped once more.

The door cracked open and one bulbous eye peered out at Gage from a narrow space between the jamb and the door. A fraction of a second later, the door swung wide. A rough hand grabbed Gage by the collar and yanked him inside. The door slammed shut behind him.

"Ow." Gage stumbled into the front room and nearly fell flat on his face. The cottage's owner, a rough looking man, peered at him out of his one good eye, the other—the one he claimed he'd lost fighting a band of blood thirsty freebooters at sea— hiding behind a stained leather patch.

"To what do I owe the pleasure of a visit from the Lostuns' Second?" Tinker folded his muscled arms over his chest.

"Aw, Tink." Gage pulled his most charming smile. "You're not still grudging me, are you?"

"Who, me?" The gruff man puffed out his breath to blow a strand of graying hair from in front of his eye. "Now, why would I be holding a grudge against such a fine and upstanding lad as yourself? Just because we made an honest deal and my payment came up short by a full quarter weight?" He squinted at Gage. "Bygones and all, eh, Gage?"

Gage grinned. "I'm glad you can see it like that, Tink."

"Oh, aye." The old man nodded, but his face turned sour. "As soon as you make up the weight. *Double.* Then we'll call it bygones."

"Double?" Gage yelped. "You're not serious?"

"Interest, lad." Tinker smiled, exposing a mouthful of broken teeth. "You owe me interest." His voice lowered. "And I'm dead serious." He lumbered across the room, sank into his chair, and turned to glare at Gage with his bloodshot eye. "Much as I like doing business with you, lad, can't have it getting about that I can be taken for a sliver nor a cog." He pulled out a gleaming knife and jabbed it into the wooden table beside him. "Wouldn't be good for trade. D'ya take my meaning?"

Gage tried not to show his dismay. He would have argued further, but he knew better than to get on Tinker's bad side. "A'course, Tink."

"Good," the old man said. "Now, that's settled, what have you brought me?"

Gage slung the sack onto the table, careful not to get too close to Tinker's razor-sharp blade. "Prime stuff." He opened his sack and spilled out the contents.

Tinker leaned forward, pawing through the items on the table. "Prime? Not as of late."

Gage reached over to pick up his breather, but Tinker smacked his hand aside. Then he picked up the end of the silver chain, pulling it from the pile of items. "Where's the fancy bobber that was attached to this?" Tinker raised his eyebrow as the chain dangled between them.

Should have known better than to offer it outright, Gage thought. "It wasn't worth clipping," he said quickly. "Broken bit of silvered trash." He shrugged, as if embarrassed to have nipped the watch in the first place.

Tinker eyed the chain, twisting it this way and that. "What a shame. Must have had somewhat of a more personal value to the owner then, to have hung it from such a fine bit as this." He considered Gage. "If I had a watch to match this, I'd likely be willing to clear a person's full debt with it, with mayhap a wee bit left over." He cleared his throat. "That is if it was a clear match for this shiny bit."

Gage hesitated. He'd been hoping to save that watch as part of his escape kit, but if it might help find Shims and the others..."Something that fine"—he licked his lips, watching for Tinker to give himself away—"surely must be worth more than that. Say, a clear debt plus a double brass weight's worth?"

"Oh, I doubt it would be worth that much." There it was. The old man's tell. His nostrils flaring just the tiniest bit as he dropped the chain back onto the pile of ill-gotten goods.

Gage shrugged, but his palms grew moist in nervous anticipation. He needed to be sly now and not give everything away.

"Tell you what," Tinker drawled. "The whole pile here, plus you find and deliver that watch to me and I'll give you the clear plus an iron weight's worth." He fingered the hilt of the knife that still jutted from the table. "And we'll forget you ever tried to pull one over on your old friend."

Gage stiffened. "Not much of a bargain." He wiped his sweaty palms against his pant legs.

Tinker laughed. "Depends on how much you value yourself, lad."

Gage couldn't argue with him on that. But letting the watch go...that would set him back hard. Ship's passage to the Southerns wasn't cheap, and he knew better than to sign on as crew to any of the working ships. Like to be caught either smuggling or pirating if the Captain was a blackguard. And if he wasn't... Well, they were all blackguards. "I'll see what I can do to acquire something to match the fob," he said, the words practically choking him.

"Good lad," Tinker said, patting him on the shoulder. "I should expect to see you again by sundown tomorrow, then?"

Gage opened his mouth to argue, but Tinker's jaw was set.

"Good, good." Tinker waved at the door, signaling it was time for Gage to leave.

"Wait," Gage said. "I need information."

"Hmmm?" Tinker eyed the small pile of valuables. "But this is barely payment for what you already owe me." He waved at the trinkets.

"There's some bloody good stuff there," Gage blurted. "And I need to know about the missing Lostuns."

"What you goin' on about?"

"My mates...some of them have gone missing. I need to know if you've any idea where they've got to."

Tinker's shoulders grew rigid. "You're not accusing old Tinker of anything criminal, are ya?" He yanked the knife from the table and slammed it into the wood again, sending splinters flying.

20

Gage licked his lips and shoved his hands in his pockets to stop them from shaking. "Naw, naw, nothin' like that, Tink. I just thought as maybe you might have heard somethin', that's all. Never mind. It's not important. I was only just askin'."

"Well, boy, ye'd best stop askin'."

He knows something. Gage started in surprise and let his blank mask slip.

Tinker scowled, then turned on his heel and grabbed Gage's bag, sweeping the pile of items from the table into it and shoving the sack at Gage. "On second thought," he said. "I've no use for any of this. No use for the troubles you're trying to bring to my fine establishment."

He opened the door, shoved Gage out onto the porch, and slammed it shut behind him.

Startled, Gage stood on the stoop, cringing at the sound of the bolt being thrown behind him. What in the ding-dang clogged nozzles was that about?

A shriveled man in a faded coat trudged by, hunching over a small sack. Probably the poor man's meager dinner. Gage hefted his own sack, wishing it contained something edible. He glanced back at Tinker's door. The old sod hadn't told him anything.

Or had he?

Tinker's refusal to talk about the disappearances had to mean something, but what? Something he should mull over somewhere other than lollybagging on Tinker's doorstep, he realized, when the old man who had passed by glanced back at him with snaky eyes.

Gage leapt off the weathered stoop, once more avoiding the rickety second step. Wouldn't do to break his neck. Nor did he care to enrich the mulish Tinker by dying on his porch with a bag of loot. Not that it was worth all that much, but it was practically all the wealth Gage had in the world. His only claim to worth aside from his pack.

He headed back down the twisting lane. It was full night now, and shadows filled the narrow street. The only light that shone came from the feeble candles that flickered through the broken shutters of the houses. None of the street lamps had been lit. Like as not, the oil had been pinched to fuel a cook fire in one of the nearby shabby dwellings.

In the better parts of town, gas lamps blazed and the scent of fresh bread and searing meat wafted into the smoky night. But not here. Here, Gage thought sourly, this is where burnt-out wishing stars fell to the earth to scorch the already soot-blackened ground.

He scuffed his boots against the rough street as he walked, wishing for a stone to kick. Then laughed at himself. Why waste a wish on a stone when he could just as easily waste it on a thick hunk of bread slathered with butter served up with a huge bowl of stew. His mouth watered at the thought. Pah. Neither was as likely as the other to come true, any rate.

He headed for the far side of Lostuns' turf where they served rough bread and weak tea, and sometimes a thin gruel, out the back door of St. Petra's, along with an overlarge portion of fiery preaching. Gage hated their talk of hellfire and sulphur as punishment for sins. Sins like thieving and pickpocketing. His throat tightened. *A wayward gent's gotta do what he's gotta do,* Checks's voice echoed in his head. As much as he hated it, as much as Mam would have hated it, there weren't much better roads for him. He pressed his fingers to his eyes to keep them from spilling his feels into the world. No place for that ninny business, Checks would say. Gage knew there weren't nothing ninny-like 'bout missing and mourning, but he also needed to keep his wits about him out in the open outside his main turf.

Anyhow, gobbling grub at St. Petra's might come with a serving of shame, but Nobs would be there sweeping up and helping out for an extra crust. One the skinny boy'd like as not give to the first hungry-looking person, or animal, he saw. But Gage owed Nobs for leading Cutter off him. And 'haps he could find some way to thank him. He might not be able to wish up a stew, but he could find a hot mug of weak tea and at least a bit of bread over at the mission. That was if he hurried.

Chapter Four
Balderdash and Poppycock

Wynd slipped along the smoky street, avoiding the jostling men and women headed to work or home from the factories, or running evening errands for wealthy employers who lived high up above the dankest streets of lower Landings. She sent a wistful glance uphill, remembering the cleaner air and the feel of soft sheets and, especially, the fullness of her belly after a good hot meal.

"Oy, watch where yer goin'," a large man groused, stumbling to sidestep and avoid tripping over her. His voice was muffled beneath his filtering mask, but a few heads still turned their way, glaring at her ragged clothes and dirt-smirched face.

Probably think I'm trying to poach them.

She couldn't blame them, since that's exactly what she'd normally be doing out on a crowded street. She lowered her head and scurfed away, doing her best to keep from being noticed any more than her bumbling daydreaming had already caused.

Stay awake, Wynd, or you're liable to be snapped up and taken to the workhouse. And then what will become of Jasp and Micah? Bad enough they'd gotten separated when the gang had been chased from their most prized bolt-hole by old Cutter. But then she'd lost sight of them, and not been able to find them... *You were supposed to look after them,* she scolded. *You promised.* She dug her ragged fingernails into her palms, snapping herself back to the present before she could fall back into that dark memory. She needed to keep her wits about her. Especially, now that she'd cut ties with the Dartlings to go after her brothers. She rubbed her knuckles across the fresh bruise she knew would already be darkening her jaw. That Buller could swing a mean fist, but she'd managed to give him something to think about. Fool still underestimated her because of her size, and like as not for being a girl. The thick-hided grunt. Though, now she'd have to find a new stick to sharpen.

Her eyes darted to and fro. No longer a member of any gang, she had to stay alert for danger from every side. It was hard to watch your own back, but she had no choice. She'd made her decision when the gang refused to help find her brothers. And there was no going back.

She picked up her pace, careful to dodge and duck around the burly men and puckery-faced women with their heads bowed and their heavy shopping buckets banging at their sides. As tempting as it might be to try and pinch a bit of bread or some other morsel from one of them, she couldn't afford to draw any more unwanted attention. Especially now that the streets were clearing. Second shift had already begun, and those left on the streets were in a hurry to get back to the comfort and safety of their own lodgings, whether a boarding house, a soldier's billet, a servant's room, or a lowly hovel. They all seemed to have places to go.

Everyone except Wynd.

The truly destitute would begin to emerge later, once they were turned out from the tea houses and soup kitchens. Wynd shuddered. She wouldn't be out at all this time of day, if things hadn't gone against her at every turn of late. Buller finding her in the bolt-hole just after she'd settled had been the least of it. Everywhere she turned she was set upon. And everywhere she'd searched for Jasp and Micah had been a dead end. There wasn't much left for her to do, but to head deeper into the worst part of Dartlings' turf and talk to Her.

The Whisperer.

Wynd knew most people, including most of the Dartlings, thought the old woman was crazy. They said her years on the streets and the thumpings she'd taken from the coppers over time had shifted something in her brain so she no longer knew real from imagined. But there were just as many who told stories of how the old woman had been right. Dead right, in some cases. That she saw things no one else could see. Things far off in time and distance.

Wynd knew what her father would have said. "Balderdash and poppycock."

But Father wasn't here. He'd climbed aboard that ship...

Wynd recalled the cold shiver that had run through her as he'd walked up the gangplank and turned to wave at them. She'd tried to run after him. To make him stay, but their mother had just pulled them all closer to huddle against the chill wind. "He'll be back afore long," Mother had said. "He'll come back and we'll all have a fine holiday supper together."

But he hadn't come back. And there'd been no

more holiday suppers. Not for any of them.

She had tried to put that day out of her mind. To tell herself that no one could know the future. It had only been the chill wind. But now she needed to see beyond what she knew. And to do that, she needed to believe.

Chapter Five
Betwixt and Between

Gage wound his way toward St. Petra's, careful to keep his collar pulled up around his ears. He'd somehow managed to make it all the way to Tinker's place without bumping into any rival gang members. Though, it had been for next to nothing. He was just thinking his luck would hold, when he heard footsteps padding behind him.

He shifted the sack of goods on his shoulder and walked steadily through the darkened street. Could be nothing. But then, why would today be different from any other day of his wretched life? He kept his head down and forced himself to keep his pace steady, so whoever was trailing him wouldn't know he'd heard. If he could just make it out of Twister's Lane and back to Lostuns turf, he might be able to outrun his pursuer. Maybe dodge into one of his pack's less used bolt-holes or duck into one of their hideys. Though they didn't have many of those anymore.

Hannigan's works would be closest. Old Hannigan would sometimes let them come in round back and sweep up his clockwork assembly room at the end of day. Even let them keep some of the shavings. But Gage doubted Hannigan would appreciate one of the Lostuns popping in with a tail, even if his main daylight work was on the up and up. Plus, after nightfall, who knew what dodgy characters might show up to avail Hands Hannigan of his darker skills. Gage shivered, remembering the steam-powered rifle Hannigan had built for one of his "special" clients a few weeks back.

That night, the old assembler had tossed Gage out on his ear before he'd even finished sweeping up the day's scraps, flipping him a thin copper for cleaning up, and making it clear that Gage was to make himself scarcer than the remaining hair on Hannigan's bald head. Only Gage's curiosity had kept him from doing as he was told. A particularly bad habit, Checks always said.

He'd hidden outside, sneaking around the building till he found a stack of crates piled neat as you please right outside a high window at the back of the assembly shop. As cautious as could be, he'd climbed the crates, moving so as not to unbalance anything, until he could grab hold of the grimy window ledge and peer through the filthy pane.

Down below, Hannigan was showing something to his visitor, a tall man in a fancy hat, with long black hair. Another man, shorter, rounder, and more than a bit bow-legged, hovered nearby. Gage never got a look at either of their faces, but there was something off about them. 'Course there was. If they were dealing out the back of Hannigan's after dark, they were sure to be as crooked as a bent shaft.

Hannigan opened a long narrow box and pulled out a heavy machine with a long tube sticking out on one end. The item shone in the lamplight, all gleaming polished brass and dark iron with a curved wooden handle. The assembler hefted the machine, holding it this way and that, and pointing to bits and spots, as he spoke. Gage couldn't hear what was said, but Hannigan was clearly showing off the item and explaining to the tall man how it worked. After a bit, he raised the machine to his shoulder and pointed it at a lumpy straw dummy hanging at the far end of the room.

The machine let out a hiss like a locomotive, followed by a roar and the sudden explosion of straw bits flying everywhere. Hannigan's visitor nodded. He reached for the machine, aimed it at a wooden dousing barrel and, with another hiss and roar, a hole erupted in the side of the cask and water poured out.

Hannigan looked unhappy, and Gage was surprised when he didn't immediately cuff the man as he would have done one of the Lostuns had they destroyed anything in the machine works. Instead, he smiled stiffly and held out his hand to take back the high-powered weapon.

The other man hesitated. After a long moment, he whipped his long hair back and handed the machine to the assembler. Some of the tension slid off Hannigan's face and shoulders, though not all. The other man said something, gesturing at the weapon. Hannigan shook his head as they haggled over price, but the assembler gave in well sooner than he would have with most of his dealings. If Hannigan was that afeared of his potential customer, it meant the tall man was worse'n his usual buyers. That were a sure signal for Gage to skedaddle afore he got caught.

He picked his way down the stack of crates, but his ragged pants caught on a nail. The boxes teetered as he tried to free himself. The shifting crates made a whuff of sound as they settled back into place.

Gage held his breath and kept his head down, crouching in the shadows in hope that if the men inside had heard and came out to look around, they might mistake a raggedy boy for a raggedy pile of trash.

But no one came.

The alley had stayed quiet, and so had Gage until long after Hannigan's nighttime visitor had slunk away into the darkness.

The following footsteps grew louder, drawing his attention back to the now, and making his decision for him. Hannigan's wouldn't do. Not tonight. Gage needed someplace else to hole up. Someplace close by.

He kept his pace steady, lest he give the stalker a reason to pounce. Up ahead, thicker shadows loomed at the end of the crooked street. Gage eyed the narrow houses on either side of the lane. Might he be able to duck between and shimmy into darkness? Or would he end up trapped in a too-narrow space or another dead end with no escape? *Think!* He pushed down the panic that turned his innards squishy. He laid out the map of Tinker's street in his mind and tried to recall the best places to shinny through, but he'd let his thoughts wander and had lost count of the buildings he'd passed.

His fist gripped the neck of his loot bag tighter. The rough burlap caught on his ragged nails. It wasn't much, and the weight of his small pile of loot was pitiful, but he could swing it hard and that was at least something. He kept walking toward the dark patch ahead.

Chapter Six
Whispers in the Dark

Wynd turned the corner and spied the crooked alley where the old woman made her bed. She glanced both ways down the narrow lane before slinking across. She couldn't afford to be seen. Escaping from Buller had cost Wynd her only weapon. She could always make another. Find another bit of wood to shape against the hard brick of one of the sturdier buildings. There were plenty of broken pallets and crates scattered about the alleyways, and even some of the worst of the lanes. Like this one. But that would take time. She slipped into the shadows, put her back to the nearest wall, and eyed the filthy roadway. None but the poorest wandered here. Them and the thugs that preyed on the dregs.

Worst of the worst.

A tinny rattle echoed out of the alley followed by the sound of someone singing. A low grating voice that clutched at the sound of music. A measured refrain that repeated over and over with barely a pause for breath. Wynd hovered, limbs abuzz with pent-up fear as she wavered between entering the alley and heading back the way she'd come.

"Where will you go, little lamb?" someone croaked.

Wynd froze.

The singing had stopped and the scratchy voice called out to her again. "Where in the starry wide world?"

Wynd gulped and stepped forward into the narrow alley.

Deep shadow clung to everything and a chill reached out and gripped her with frigid fingers.

A dusky figure stepped out of the murky shadows. "Those who hover near my habitation," the figure said, "must propose their purpose." A pale hand reached out, lifted a dented tin, shook it, then tossed it aside.

"Um, Whisp-Whisp-Whisp..." Wynd stammered.

"For what purpose do the stars propose a question to be answered?" The figure turned on her of a sudden, sunken eyes gleaming. "What souvenir have you shifted for old Whisp-Whisp-Whisperer from the far-flung reaches of the sky?"

Wynd froze. Her hand crept up to the string around her neck. Her fingers clutched the trinket tied there. The only thing left. The last of the charms. The tiny star her father had given her right before he'd left.

"You're my North star, Wynd. You, your mother, and your brothers," he'd said as he clipped the silver star onto her charm bracelet. "You'll always lead me home."

But they hadn't, had they?

Wynd had parted with the other charms. For bread, and clothing, and even a bit of soup. Till none had been left but the little star.

Had the old woman seen it? Is that why she'd said what she had? But, no. How could she? It was dark, and the tiny star lay nestled against Wynd's skin, hidden beneath her shirt.

Most people scoffed at the idea that the Whisperer could see things no one else could. But some said the Whisperer had been right too many times to ignore. She knew things. Could tell you things. For a price. And right now, no price was too great. Not if it helped Wynd keep her promise. Not if it meant finding Jasp and Micah.

Chapter Seven
Hide and Seek

Gage tensed, preparing to dodge off the lane and into the space between two shuttered houses when a dark silhouette separated itself from the gloom in front of him. Cutter! He froze mid-step. The scuttling footfalls drew closer, but he dared not turn to look behind him. Not with the figure of Constable Cutter looming ahead.

"Thought you'd got away?" Cutter sucked in a mouthful of phlegm and spat it out onto the already filthy street, then made a wet smacking sound.

Ugh.

Gage's knees shook. He stood tight as a rusted bolt, listening. The footsteps grew louder and faster. He needed to make a move before—Too late. His loot bag was snatched from his shoulder, the contents clanking together as the bag ripped open.

He glanced back to see a thin, raggedy boy pawing through the sack, as if searching for something. "Who're you?" he growled.

"Nunnyer biznezz." The skinny boy barely glanced a side-eye up at him.

"Oy!" hollered Cutter, taking a menacing step toward them. "What you think yer up to?"

The skinny boy looked up, eyes growing wide as if just noticing Cutter.

Gage saw the advantage, but before he could open his mouth, the older boy snarled and held up the sack. "He stole me goods, he did."

"Didn't!" Gage snapped back. "That's mine. You saw him lift it from me."

Cutter's face grew dark. "Naw. All mine." He sneered. "Both of youse and the bag. Pass it over." He held out one hand and raised the other, his ugly club gripped in a hairy fist.

The boy snarled again, this time showing crooked teeth. Then he swung the sack over his shoulder and sped off down the darkened lane, worn shoes slapping at the packed dirt at the edge of the road. "All yerz, Constable," he called over his shoulder. "I got me an appointment to keep down the way. Pleazure doin' biznezz."

Anger buzzed inside Gage's head. *Ding-dangit!* It was a trap. He'd been set up. Tinker had played him, that rotted piece of grizzle! He'd sent that scraggedy drip to grab up his loot. Probably let Cutter know to look for him tonight, too.

"One in the hand, then." Cutter rushed forward, swinging his club, catching Gage on the shoulder and clipping his ear. Gage ducked low and dodged sideways. Pain seared and his ear rang. Cutter came at him again and Gage leaped away, springing into the shadows between two broken-down buildings.

Deeper darkness enveloped him as he ran, his eyes searching ahead for dead ends and barriers. Behind him, Cutter shouted and huffed, but he'd been slow to follow Gage into the shadows. Too many ways to be ambushed in the dark, especially in a section of town like Twister's Lane. The sudden thought of what might be lurking in the darkness slowed Gage, but not before he tripped over something low and jagged that tore at his breeches and clawed at his shins. He nearly screamed at the feel of the jagged teeth that gnawed at his leg before realizing it was just a rusted row of cogs attached to some sort of axle. It leaned at a low angle in a shallow ditch, sparse dried weeds clinging between metal wheels. The space beneath the upper end was narrow and dark, but Cutter was still coming, picking his way in the gloom.

Gage dove beneath the broken metal and rolled as far under as he could. Maybe, just maybe, he'd get lucky and Cutter would keep going and pass him by. But luck sure hadn't been a friend of late.

He held his breath.

Chapter Eight
Dock and Cover

Deep in the center of Dockers' turf, a weathered warehouse stood guard at the end of a sagging dock. Though the exterior of the building was old and in disrepair, inside there burned a glowing fire day and night. Its flames fed the boilers of the largest smuggling operation in Landings. Small boats crewed by rough-looking men tied up to the dock beside the warehouse at all hours.

Money changed hands. Teams of haulers unloaded the boxes and barrels that arrived. Then, the boats would cast off and head back out through the constant clouds of mist, with only the plash of oars to mark their passing. The Dockers were well paid to guard the warehouse and protect its secrets. Nosy snoopers had been known to make a splash of their own, a very final one, if the gang caught them getting too close.

Wynd was well aware of the danger, but she was bound and determined to find Jasp and Micah. And the information Whisperer had offered up—such as it was—had led her here.

She slipped from shadow to shadow, pausing each time to slow her heart and open her ears and her nose. She had a great capacity to smell not only danger, but people. Especially those who bathed as seldom as the Dockers gang. She wrinkled her nose in distaste. Some would say a strong sense of smell might be a detriment to a street urchin, but Wynd trusted her skills to keep her alive. Her ears and nose had never failed her.

Faintly, off along the dock, she thought she heard the tell-tale ticking of a clock, but that made no sense. *Tick-tick. Tick-tick.* The sound came again and she perked up her ears. A pocket watch would have to be quite near for even her sensitive ears to hear. And a clock!?! No one would be carrying a clock along the docks at night. Not unless they were looking to get squeezed and fleeced.

She tucked herself into a tight cranny between a weathered crate and the outer wall of the warehouse and held her breath to better hear what made the muffled ticking sound. Along with it, grew the sound of voices speaking quietly. As they came closer, the ticking grew, and over that Wynd could just make out the words being spoken.

"I tell you, Jukes," a man's voice said. "This is the slickest scheme Cap'n Spindle has come up with yet."

"I dunno 'bout that, Mullsy," came another man's voice. This one sounded like someone with a perpetual stuffy nose. "'Member the time—"

"Shut it. You've no idea what you're talking about," the first man said. "Never did a finer plan develop in our Cap'n's brain. This scheme will make us all filthy rich."

"But what if someone comes looking for them?"

Stuffy nose sounded worried.

"Hah! That's the beauty of it, ain't it? No one cares what happens to a bunch of runny-nosed streeters."

Streeters? Wynd nearly gasped. Did they mean Micah and Jasp?

She was keen to get a look at the men attached to the voices, but their conversation began to recede again without passing by her hidey, and the strange ticking went with them. *Cog rust!* She eased herself out of the hidey and picked her way to the corner of the building to peer around it for a sight of the men. She leaned forward, prepared to follow them, and froze at the scent of a Docker. How it could be a point of pride for anyone not to bathe was a riddle she'd rather not delve into. But to make it a gang oath? And for members to be willing to swear it? There wasn't enough gold in the crown's coffers! But it made for an excellent early warning.

She stayed still in the shadows, hoping against hope she was mistaken, that someone had left dead fish guts to rot on the wharf, or a broken chamber pot. But no, there was no mistaking that stench and it was coming nearer by the second. She backed away, only to be assaulted by the smell of another of the notorious gang members coming from behind her. She glanced about frantically, looking for another place to hide, but there was nowhere to go. She was trapped on the dock in Dockers' territory, standing outside their most guarded secret, and they were coming her way.

There was no place to run and no place to hide. Nowhere but the filthy bay. She stared at the dark water.

Not that.

Her fists clenched and her body shook. Anything would be preferable to ducking herself into the same salty water that had taken her father. Even getting caught by a bunch of stinking Dockers on their turf. Only, she'd made a promise. She had promised to watch over Micah and Jasp. And to do that, she had to find them.

There was nothing else for it. She crept to the edge of the rotted dock, gritted her teeth, and shimmied down a slimy post, sliding as quietly as possible into the cold dark water. She clung to the wood piling, heart beating like the slamming of a broken cog wheel, telling herself over and over that she could do this.

She could do anything, if it meant finding Micah and Jasp.

Chapter Nine
Bitey-Bugs

"No use hiding," Cutter called into the gloom. The sound of his heavy boots stomped nearer, then moved past.

Gage stayed quiet, trying to slow the thud-thud-thud of his pounding heart after the run he'd made. It was all he could do not to breathe like a wheezy old steamer engine.

Cutter's footsteps circled back. Gage held his breath and stayed as still as a seized cylinder.

"Might go easier on you if you was to give up and come along quiet-like," Cutter said, then busted out a laugh. "Good one, Cutter," he muttered. "Pah. I need a drink." His footsteps moved away again, and Gage took in a slow-slow breath.

"Only a matter of time before I catch up with you. Ever' stinking one." Cutter's voice grew distant as he picked his way past the junk strewn between the empty buildings and out into the next narrow lane. "You're all going to the pits."

Gage lay in the dark a long time to be sure Cutter wasn't just lying in wait for him to come out. The constable wasn't known for his patience, but like Checks always said, 'A careless rat is a dead rat.' Best to stay ducked and covered for a bit. But as he lay there, mourning the loss of his loot, something pinched at his side. *Ow!* Just what he needed, some kind of stinking bitey-bug gnawing on him. He tried to ignore it, but it was too big and too annoying. It scratched its way up his ribs till he couldn't stand it anymore. He squeezed his arm against his side, hoping it was squishable, but it only pinched harder. "Ow." He slapped a hand over his mouth. Hopefully, Cutter had gone in search of that drink instead of lurking about in wait. Whatever it was inside his shirt was clearly not squishable and buzzed against his ribs like a misaligned gear.

He eased the pressure and rolled his weight off the thing, hoping it would simply crawl away. The biting and scratching stopped, but the hard edges of the creature stayed put. Oy. What was it? It didn't feel like it had latched on like a tick or a leech. Yet. What if it was fixing to lay eggs and plant its buggy get on him? He needed to rid hisself of the thing. He needed someplace with light to make sure.

He squiggled out from under the mechanical mess and crept to the edge of the quiet lane. All clear. He slid through the shadows, close and silent, trying not to rouse the bug that still clung to his skin beneath his ragged shirt. Last thing he wanted was to wake it from its stillness. If he could skitter back to Lostuns' turf without disturbing it, he might be able to prise it off without causing rumination to his carcass.

Chapter Ten
Neck-Deep

Wynd clung to a bit of rotted rope that hung from the dock while keeping her head as far out of the greasy water as possible. She tried not to think about her parents. How her father must have worried for them even as the storm sank his ship. How her mother had tried to go on, but then had become lost, curling up inside her own despair.

She pushed away the dark memories and tried not to think about the nasty refuse and waste that fouled the bay, and the vast sea licking her chin. Would there were such a thing as a breather that could filter water. Though, even if such a thing were possible, she'd not be able to afford it. When she'd left the Dartlings, they hadn't even let her keep the breather she'd worked so hard for. Said it was gang-got goods and she was no longer entitled to it. Blocks had yanked it from her grip and tossed her a half-used filter rag. And that was now a sodden mess hanging round her neck.

The cold, dark water sucked the warmth from her, taunting her. *I took your father*, it seemed to say. *Took your mother, too, in the end. And I'll take you.* A nearby splash startled her, and her grip slipped on the slimy rope. Her face went under up to her eyes. She popped back up, barely able to keep from spluttering, and clutched the rope more tightly than she'd have gripped a shiny farthing. She shut her lips tight. Any sound might give her away. Besides, better not to swallow any of the nasty seawater.

Overhead, voices muttered and a match was struck, hissing as it burned to life. Wynd froze. If she could hear someone lighting a match, they could surely hear any movement she made. If they heard her, she'd be lucky to keep her hide intact.

The splash had come from behind her. With nary a sound, she turned her body round to search the dark water for whatever had caused the noise. Probably just some dock scum tossing an empty bottle into the sea. But it hadn't sounded like a bottle. It had sounded more like something had slapped the water. With a tail. Or a tentacle. Wynd shivered. Stories of sea monsters raced through her panicky brain. *Stop it*, she told herself. *This is no time to be thinking of monsters.*

An unbidden memory of her father checking under her bed and in the wardrobe bubbled up and she tried to quell it before the memories she knew would follow could reach her, but it was too late. The images rose in her mind. Father putting a hand on her shoulder bidding her to look after her brothers while he was away. Her mother's cry of grief as she collapsed to the floor, the tele-ticker note clutched in her hand. The heart-breaking words: *Lost at sea. No trace found.* Mother struggling to make ends meet. The way she tried, only to fail, leaving them with more debt than they could pay. Mother turning their dog, Flecks, out into the streets. Jasp and Micah's running after.

Wynd had tried to find them and bring them home. But by the time she'd tracked them, there was no home to return to.

Mother was gone.

Wynd stifled the cry of pain and anger that threatened to escape her lips. How could she? Hadn't Wynd sworn to bring the boys home? Hadn't she kept her promise? But Mother, their dear, broken Mother had left them, anyway. Left them to fend for themselves.

Wynd had sworn she would care for her brothers, had promised, but now it appeared she was to be denied even that.

The bitter stench of burning tobacco wafted down to her. They were still there. What were they waiting for? Why wouldn't they leave?

From a short distance across the water came the quiet plashing of oars manned by rowers intent on maintaining silence. *Brittle pins!* She had the worst of luck. Of course, she'd end up right in the middle of a nighttime smuggling operation. Always the most dangerous kind.

Stealthily, she shifted her handhold on the rope and inched around, easing herself behind the thick wooden dock post. There was barely room for her to keep her face above water even with the top of her head smooshed up against the filthy underside of the dock, but she forced herself to keep going. Was it already high tide? Or would the water rise up to cover her completely? She shivered at the thought.

The rotted piling she clung to was covered in oozy slime and razor-sharp barnacles that threatened to slit open her hands at the lightest touch. She knew better than to let blood flow into these murky waters. She'd heard the stories of what rose up to gobble the chum tossed out by fishermen, who brought back their small catches and cleaned them on the docks before heading home for the night.

The boat drew nearer, a silhouette containing darker man-shaped shadows that formed against the dark night. They drifted closer, blocking out the few stars that penetrated the murky sky. Wynd held her breath, putting the thick post between her and the oncoming boat. It was so close now she could hear the creaking of the oars in their locks and the hard breathing of the men who pulled at them.

A sudden flash of light flared above and was quickly cut off. A beacon to bring them to the correct berth. Dicey. That the men on the docks would risk it meant the smuggled cargo must be valuable. Wynd steeled herself and remained silent as the boat bumped up against the dock directly beside the narrow pile she hid behind. Were the water any lower and the night any brighter, the men aboard the craft might have been able to glimpse a pair of eyes peering up between the planks of the dock where they tossed up the lines.

Above her, the ropes were made fast and the boat quickly unloaded. Boxes were handed off, the only sound the grunts of the men as they heaved the crates of ill-gotten goods onto the dock.

"That's the lot," a gruff voice said from the boat.

"Not by my tally," came the response.

"Then you'd better count again," another voice said from the boat.

"You're short," the man on the dock accused.

"That's a fine statement coming from one as likes to cheat even more 'en he likes to drink."

Quiet laughter erupted on the boat.

"You'd cheat your own mother, if you had one."

"Why not?" The man on the boat retorted. "I cheated yours."

More laughter spilled out of the boat.

"Shut your yaps!" Heavy boots stomped to the edge of the dock. All laughter died as if cut off with a knife. "As for you, I'll slit you from gullet to gut, if you ever say another word about me mother." A man coughed and, with a thud, the boat rocked, sending a ripple of waves over Wynd's face. "When I say you're short, you're short. And I'd better be seeing the rest of the Cap'n's cargo on the next delivery. D'ya undertake my meaning?"

"Aye," the other man rasped unhappily. "I'll pass on your message to Yoahn the Waster," he said, then lowered his voice to grumble. "We'll see what he thinks of your meaning."

Wynd cringed. Yoahn the Waster was a notorious buccaneer, who was said to be able to pass on the rotting disease to anyone who crossed him. It was also said that his own face had rotted away to the point that he had no ears and his nose was naught but a hole in the middle of his face.

"There's worse onna sea than Yoahn," the first man muttered.

Wynd shivered, the chill reaching deep inside her. She clenched her jaw tight to keep her teeth from chattering. Then realized with a start that the water had risen above her chin. Her pulse pounded frantically against her ribs, and her breath caught in her throat. The tide was still coming in, and she was trapped beneath this rotten dock!

Chapter Eleven
Buckets of Bad Luck

By the time Gage made it back to Lostuns' turf, it was the twee hours of the morning. None but the busiest of factories were running at this hour and the Nest would be dark and crowded with skinny bodies all jostling for warmth and trying to find the peace of sleep. He'd managed to make it this far without disruptering the crawly inside his shirt, but Checks would knock him into last year if he brought something nasty into the Nest and woke the gang to boot. He needed somewhere to inspect the thing that still clung to his ribs beneath his tattered shirt and jacket. And he needed to make sure it hadn't tucked anything under his skin. That's a thing he *didn't* need. An explosion of vermin growing inside his chest. He needed somewhere with light, but no curious nosers to bother with. He snuck around the looming warehouses and into the narrow back alley three buildings down from the gear works.

At the back of a greasy building, a dark doorway

held the exact place. The janitor's shop hugged the back corner of the Parnell Pipeworks. Pipers only worked two shifts, with the dead hours of the night set aside for mechanical maintenance and cleaning up the debris from the day's work. Or so the schedule said. Gage knew that the current janitor would have slipped off by now to tip a bottle with one of his cronies. After a quick look about and a long listen, he worked at the loose lock till the knob turned in his hand and the door swung open.

The gloom-filled room stank of rotting rags and mold, but Gage was used to worse. He slipped inside the windowless space and located the nearest oil lamp before swinging the door shut behind him. His fingers slid along the edge of the lamp until they found the box of matches he knew would be there. The light of the match glared against the darkness and when he touched it to the lantern's wick, the shadows in the room gave way.

The space was a crowded mess of broom handles and old rags. Buckets and brushes sat heaped on benches and hung from rusty spikes jutting from the walls at random angles. But none of that interested Gage. Slowly, carefully, he slipped off his jacket, set it on a nearby workbench, raised his shirt and peered down at...nothing?

That couldn't be right. It had just been there, clinging beneath his shirt, scraping against his ribs. He could see the red scratches where it had broken the skin. Ugh. There were no punctures, thank the stars, and at least it was off him now. But what was it? And where had it got to?

He reached for his jacket but stepped back when it gave a small shudder. The blasted thing had somehow latched onto his jacket when he'd taken it off. Well, it was trapped now, beneath the ragged fabric. All he had to do was lift his jacket up and slap a bucket down over the thing and it would be the janitor's problem next day. Too bad Gage wouldn't be around to see what it was. Though, he could maybe loiter nearby when the next janitor's shift started. Might be worth a good laugh.

He grabbed a bucket, reached over and slammed it upside down onto the workbench. "Gotcha!"

A muffled buzzing came from inside the bucket, which started to rock and inch toward the edge of the workbench. "No ya don't." Gage shoved the bucket back and held it down, glancing around the room for something heavy to place on it. He stepped away to grab a small crate filled with scrapers and brushes, but the bucket bucked and rocked as soon as he let go. "Set still, will ya?"

The bucket quieted. Gage slowly drew his hand away and eyed the grimy wooden pail. Sneaky as could be, he took a step away and then another, edging toward the crate. But as soon as he'd picked up the box of tools, the bucket on the bench inched toward the edge again. He swung back around, but in his haste, tripped over a pile of rags and went sprawling. The box and all its contents spilled across the floor with a crash. Gage quickly gathered what he could back into the box and slapped it on top of the bucket, hoping no one had heard the noise. Last thing he needed was to get cornered in a filthy cleaning closet.

The muffled buzzing and knocking went on inside the bucket, but the weight of the tools was enough to keep it in place. Finally, the captured creature quieted. Gage dusted his palms in satisfaction, then stopped. He stared at the tattered cuff that stuck out from under the edge of his makeshift trap. "Naw," he muttered. "Naw, naw, naw."

His ding-dang jacket. It was still under the bucket. He hadn't felt the cold while he was busy trying to find a way to keep the insect in its place. But now, he shivered in the chill damp. It was late in the year and the weather was getting colder. He couldn't be without a jacket. And the one beneath the bucket, patched and dirty as it was, was the only one he owned. He had to retrieve it.

Chapter Twelve
A Big Splash

Moving as silent as she could, Wynd fought her panicking brain and reached up with shaking hands. Her fingers slipped on the slimy boards, coming away covered in long greasy strands. She ignored the awful feel and traced along the slippery wood until she found a frayed bit of rope. She gripped onto it and pulled herself deeper under the dock. If she moved far enough from the smugglers, she might be able to escape from beneath the rotting structure and the rising waters that had reached her mouth. She tilted her head back and closed her eyes, fighting her revulsion as thick strands of the slimy substance dragged across her face.

Slow and quiet, she pulled herself along, hoping she was aimed in the right direction. Fearing she might veer off target, she paused to open her eyes to small slits to try and get her bearings.

Something cold slithered against her legs. A strange whirring and ticking rose up from below.

She gasped, sucked in a mouthful of nasty seawater, and froze.

Above her, a voice hissed, "What was that?"

"Dunno," came an answer. "Rats?"

"Didn't sound like rats to me," someone said. "Sounded more like we've got unwanted eyes on us. Eyes that we'll pluck out when we find 'em."

Wynd held her breath as footsteps pounded across the dock above her.

"Search those barrels," the voice ordered.

"Come out, Rat," a voice called. "Show yerself and we might let you live."

The men in the boat shoved off. "You're on your own," the voice from earlier said, as oars splashed in the murky water and the small boat pulled away from the dock.

The ticking and whirring noise grew louder. Then with a splash, something glinted in the feeble starlight. A huge head with a long snout and glistening eyes peered out of the water a few feet away from the edge of the dock.

"There!" Someone called.

"What is that?"

"Looks like a...No, it can't be..."

Gears whirred and the large head snapped open, revealing rows of sharp metal teeth. A hiss of water rose from the thing's huge maw. Then, with a slurp, the scaly head ducked below the water. With the splash of a long tail, it disappeared into the dark.

"You ever seen anything like that?"

"Only ever seen or heard of salt-water crocs in the tropics. Ain't it too cold here for such a creature."

"I dunno, but I never heard of one what shined like metal."

"Get these crates off the dock," the man in charge ordered. "And then make yourselves scarce till you hear from me." His voice was commanding, but

Wynd heard a tremor of fear behind it.

"Aye-aye," the men responded and scurried to their work.

By the time their footsteps receded into the night, the water had nearly reached the dock. Wynd had no other choice, but to duck her head beneath the filthy water and pull herself as best she could to the far edge. Her head popped up from beneath the water and she panted and gasped, relieved to be out from under the oppressive space. She stared around, afraid the huge metal monster might be lurking nearby, waiting to swallow her whole. Or worse, bite her in two.

She paddled her way to the quay and pulled herself along, searching frantically for a ladder, or any way up and out of the perilous water. The image of being eaten by a sea monster filled her with strength. She pulled herself along until she reached the rocky embankment at the edge of the quay where she could grasp hold and clamber up onto the shore. She wanted nothing more than to collapse and breathe, but her better instincts sent her running and dripping into the shadows, searching for safety. She needed a dry place to hole up in for what was left of the night.

Chapter Thirteen
All That Glitters

Night was nearly done and dawn would be along soon. Gage had to get his jacket back and scarper off before the lanes and alleys filled with first-shifters on their way to work.

He stared at the overturned bucket. Maybe he could just slide the jacket out from under without disturbing anything.

He gave the cuff a gentle tug and a bit more of the sleeve slipped out from under the edge of the bucket, but the whole mess wibble-wobbled dangerously. He tried holding onto the edge of the crate while pulling at the sleeve and managed to get it out up to the shoulder before he heard a ripping sound. "Grindy-gears!" This just wasn't working and time was running out. He needed to get his jacket out from under the bucket and get himself back to the Nest, or at least wedged into a hidey before day shift. Morning hours were the worst for a streeter to be out. Not enough crowd for a good pinch and too easy to get bashed about if one didn't watch his backside. Morning shifters were always an extra crabby bunch.

"Fine." He lifted the crate off the top of the bucket and set it aside. He sucked in a deep breath, then whipped off the bucket, yanked out his jacket, and slammed the bucket back down.

Too late. The creature was out and buzzing like an angry hornet. It leaped at him. He swatted it with his jacket and sent it plummeting to the floor with a metallic clink. It lay there, glittering in the lamplight. Shiny and small. But it didn't look much like a bug. Gage tiptoed closer and leaned down to get a better look. Not a bug at all, but a tiny figure. It was made of metal, all polished and fine. He nudged it with the toe of his boot.

Nothing.

It lay as if it hadn't been buzzing and rattling and knocking about just moments ago. As if it had never moved. But it might just be playing possum. Gage clapped his hands together over the thing. Once. Twice. Nothing.

He picked it up and carried it over to the light for a better looksee. The small metal trinket, shaped like a bitty person with wings, lay on the palm of his hand. Some kind of fairy doll. He slipped on his goggles and set the lecture lens to its highest setting. It might be cracked, but it would still provide enough enlargement to give him a better view.

The delicate work was unlike anything he'd seen before. The polished surfaces and fine clockwork detail made it look like a person, tiny as it was. Gotta be something of Tinker's. Something that had somehow hitched a ride inside his jacket. But why? And why wasn't it working? Could he have damaged it when he'd swatted it with his jacket? It seemed sturdy enough. Hadn't it survived being squished between his arm and his ribs?

No matter. Something this fine must be worth more than a trifle. His spirits rose. Finally, luck had decided to give him a good turn. This was his ticket to paying off his debt and getting evened up with Tinker. Valuable as it must be, maybe the old scrounger would help him find a way out of Landings, too.

He turned the toy over in his hands, peering closely to see if something might be jamming the mechanics. Perhaps, like most things, this too was powered by steam. Though, Gage saw nothing that looked like a steam engine, or even a flow port for a steam injection. He turned the tiny key of the finely crafted clockwork. Nothing.

He flicked at the whispy wings, trying to start them flapping, but the shiny creature remained still. Maybe slamming it to the floor had damaged a gear, or dislodged something. "Better not be broken," Gage mumbled. "Tinker isn't likely to pay up a ransom if his bauble doesn't work." He tapped the little mechanical doll on the top of its head and heard a small metallic chime, like a tiny bell. He gripped the toy in his fist in frustration and something sharp stabbed into his finger. "Ow!" He dropped the trinket and stuck the tip of his finger into his mouth. "Aw, fish guts!" he shouted, stepping back to see where the toy had landed. Only, the metal fairy wasn't there. Gage turned in a slow, careful circle, afraid he might step on the fragile thing and crush it.

He made it all the way around before he heard it. A whirring and clicking just above his head. He raised his eyes. Lacy wings flapped furiously, speeding up to a blur. The clockwork fairy began to glow, rising into the air before dropping down to hover in front of him with a tinkling sound like the ringing of tiny bells.

No way this was Tinker's craftwork. Gage had

never seen anything like it. "You're really real." Spellbound, he reached for the hovering creature.

The fairy darted out of his reach and zipped across the room.

"Wait!" he cried out in alarm. "Come back!"

In a blur, it flew back across the room and hovered at eye level, as if waiting for another command.

Gage blinked in surprise. It wasn't only a mechanical wonder, but somehow it understood him. "Can you spin?"

In answer to his question, the golden wind-up twirled prettily in the air, then bobbed to a stop and took a bow.

Gage's mouth fell open. It truly was a wonder. Tinker would be like to set a fabulous finder's fee on the device. Gage rubbed his chin. "Well, then. Let's just get you back to Tinker and collect my reward, shall we?"

The fairy buzzed furiously and flew up to the corner of the room. Landing on a high beam, it shook and shivered, a cascade of jangling sounds pouring from it. If Gage hadn't known better, he'd think the mad thing was yelling at him.

He gazed up at it. "Not possible," he said. "You're nought but a mechanical bug."

In a blur, the fairy dropped from its perch, whipped out a tiny sword the size of a sewing needle, and swooped down. In a mad rush, it stabbed the tip of Gage's earlobe before soaring up and lighting on the beam near the ceiling once more.

"Ow!" Gage rubbed at his ear. His fingers came away with a smear of blood from the stinging wound. "What was that for?"

The fairy made another round of jangling noises, slammed the eensy sword into its belt and gestured at him with its tiny fists.

"So, you want to fight?"

A tinkling noise came from the creature. It sounded like laughter.

"And what's so funny about it?" Gage demanded.

The clockwork fairy dove down once more, circled Gage's head at a dizzying speed. He swatted the air, trying to knock it away, but it drove in close, plucked a hair from his head, and buzzed away in the twinkling of an eye.

"Ow!" Gage complained again.

The fairy hovered just out of reach, dropped the freshly plucked hair and dusted its wee hands together as if wiping away soil. Then it let out a fresh burst of tinkling laughter.

Gage wasn't about to give up his reward that easily. He looked around the room, searching for something he could use to capture the annoying thing. His eyes landed on a filthy mop that had been used down to its last few strands.

Trying not to appear obvious, he sauntered over to the corner where the mop leaned against a pile of empty crates. "Perhaps," he said, "we could come to some arrangement?"

The clockwork tilted its small head to show it was listening.

Gage lowered his voice. "To be blunt, I'm not particularly fond of old Tinker, myself," he said as if imparting a secret.

The fairy drew closer.

"You see," Gage said, pretending to lean on the mop handle and glancing around the room, as if someone might hear. "I've never really told anyone this..." He leaned forward as the fairy hovered nearer.

Gage grabbed the handle and whipped it through the air, aiming the ropy clumps of the mop head at the darting fairy.

The clockwork creature buzzed like an angry wasp and glowed red. It zipped through the air, dodging the swinging mop.

Gage swung again, bringing the mop around in an arc over his head. The angry buzzing grew louder. The mechanical fairy zipped in beneath the mop and stung Gage's other ear. "Ow!" He swung harder. But every swing missed.

The fairy dodged in again, taking another swipe at his other ear. Then another on the tip of his nose. "Ow. Ouch! Stop it, you blasted bug!"

Finally, Gage dropped the mop and wrapped his arms over his head, covering his face and ears. "Leave off. Leave off. Truce. Truce!"

The creature stung him once more, then the angry buzzing receded up to the roof beam in the corner of the room again. This time, the sound that came from the small thing sounded more like something banging on a bit of metal. More a sour clanking note than the ringing of chimes.

Gage raised his eyes to the beam where the fairy stood with one hand on a hip and the other pointing at him in a scolding manner.

"Are you...Are you cursing me?" Gage burst out laughing.

The fairy turned a darker shade of red and flailed both arms at him.

"Sorry. Sorry." Gage held up his hands in surrender and attempted to stifle his laughter. "Sorry for laughing." He rubbed at his nose and stared at the spot of blood that came away on his fingers. "You've a mean bite," he said, with admiration.

The glow around the little being faded from red, then flashed blue for a moment, along with a tinkling sound.

"You're welcome?" Gage thought perhaps there might be another way to deal with this creature. And perhaps even a way to better use it than to simply turn it back over to Tinker. A way that might prove even more valuable to Gage. And his mates.

"Mayhap, we really could come to an agreement," he said.

The fairy remained where it was up in the corner, out of reach, tiny metal hands on its hips. Waiting.

"I think we could work together." Gage kicked the mop into the corner and held out his hands to show they were empty. "You help me earn enough to buy me and the boys our passage out of this hole, and I'll help you stay away from that rotted Tinker."

He waited to see what reaction the small creature might offer. But the fairy remained silent and stayed where it was.

"I'd be willing to swear an oath, if you would." Gage touched his ear and held up his fingers. "Not like as if we don't have the blood for it."

The clockwork fairy struck a pose, chin on fist, as if considering the offer.

Gage grimaced, then looked thoughtful. "Would that work for you? Or do we need something else? Oil, maybe?"

The fairy flared red for a moment, then flashed blue again and let go a sliding scale of chimes.

Gage nodded. "I'll take that as a no to the oil bit. But we'll need a way to make the oath."

It slipped off the ceiling beam and dropped to the floor, landing so softly it might have been a mere pin dropping. It stood looking at Gage, as if daring him to move. Then, it scraped its wings together and a dusting of metal settled onto the floor at its feet. It drew its tiny sword and traced something in the dust. Then leaped into the air and landed on the beam once more.

Gage took a few steps forward, then bent down to get a closer look. Scratched into the floor in silver dust was the outline of a tiny bell.

"Is this like signing your name?" Gage asked.

The fairy nodded once.

"Bell? Your name's Bell?"

The fairy shook its head and made a sound.

"Jingle?" Gage guessed.

The fairy whipped out its tiny sword and Gage flinched. "Whoa, we don't need any more of that."

The clockwork swooped down and drew a clapper on the bottom of the bell with the point of the sword, let out another peal of sound, then held both hands over its ears and ducked its head.

"Oh, louder than a jingle?"

The fairy nodded in encouragement.

"Bong?"

The fairy glared and waggled its head.

"Clap?"

The fairy started and held a hand behind an ear, then stuck out the other waggling it side-to-side.

"So, sounds like Clap but not really?" Gage tapped a finger against his chin in thought. "Clang?"

The fairy waved a hand at him.

Gage closed his eyes and scrunched his face, trying to squeeze out more words, but words had always been hard for him.

Something grabbed at his collar and his eyes popped open.

The clockwork tugged at him and he inched his way across the room, following where it led. It swooped down and landed on a broken ax-blade. "Ax?"

The clockwork nodded and flew back over to the bell and pointed.

"Cla—ax?" Gage guessed.

This time the fairy nodded and flashed blue with a happy tinkle.

"Your name is Clax?"

The fairy nodded again, flashing blue at the same time.

"And you're making this your pledge?" Gage eyed the tracing on the floor.

A nod and a blue flash.

Gage kneeled on the floor, then reached up and squeezed the tip of one ear where he'd been stabbed. He held his finger over the symbol scratched into the floor and let the blood drip onto it. It sizzled as it struck the silvery dust, giving off a tiny puff of smoke that smelled of copper and the smoky sky just before a big storm. Startled, he gazed up at the fairy, who gestured for him to continue. "I give you my word," he intoned, "that if you help me and the Lostuns gain passage out of this rotted place, we will always protect you and we will keep you as one of our own." It was much the same pledge he'd made when the pack had taken him in.

A shiver went through him, as much from his committing the gang to something without leave as from the cold air that had taken on a pre-dawn bite. Checks might not like it, nor might some of the other Lostuns, but Gage didn't care. What mattered was finding a way out of this rotted city, and Clax could be just the ticket he'd been searching for. He set his jaw and rose from the floor, grabbing his torn jacket and slipping it on.

With the swiftness of a bee, the fairy swooped down and landed on Gage's shoulder. He forced himself not to cringe away, afraid the creature might stab him again. Instead, with a small tinkling sound, Clax grabbed hold of Gage's ragged collar and settled onto his shoulder like a bird on a perch.

Their pact made, Gage and Clax headed out into the night.

Chapter Fourteen
Making a Point

Wynd ground the stick against the coarse bricks, her anger fueling her work. The point was already sharper than the last one she'd made. The one she'd broken in the tussle with Buller.

She gritted her teeth. What a fool she'd been to believe in the ravings of an old woman. Idiot! She should have seen it. Of course, the Whisperer was part of a long con. How else could a lone old woman survive for so long on the worst streets in the city? Wynd recalled the way the woman's eyes had glittered in the darkness, catching the starlight...Pah! It had to be a trick.

Father had been right about such things and people as Whisperer. Poppycock and balderdash, indeed. All of it. And Wynd had fallen for it.

The old hag's so-called vision had been so vague as to be nearly useless. Unless, someone who wanted to believe put meaning into it. As Wynd had. "Across the water and above the fire." Whisperer had hissed of a sudden before adding, "Surrounded by danger."

That had gotten Wynd's attention, but the rest of it: "Feathers out of flight and flight without feather." That part made no sense. Wynd had asked her to explain, but the Whisperer had refused to answer. She'd shooed her away with a flick of a bony wrist, saying, "What am I but a candle with a flickery flame? You must find your own way through the murk."

Wynd would have stayed to argue; her silver star had been worth more than a three-line riddle! But a loud crash from the end of the alley had caused the Whisperer to stiffen, eyes widening. And in those eyes, Wynd had seen what at first had appeared to be a reflection of the starry night. But the vastness of what she'd seen in the old woman's eyes had caused her to look up and gasp. Clouds and smoke had turned the sky to inky black and nary a star glimmered above.

The fear that shivered over Wynd had sent her skittering.

Now, she was sure the noise had been a part of the con. A way to get rid of the unhappy customers who came seeking answers that were nothing of the kind. The rest of it, well, she had no idea how it was done, but rumors of séance fakers making tables float and images appear made it clear that there were plenty of ways to con the desperate. Those who would trade everything they owned for news of their family.

Her hand flew up to her neck where the star charm no longer hung. She wished she hadn't been so gullible. But wishes were for fairy stories, not for an orphan searching for two lost boys.

Chapter Fifteen
On Dangerous Ground

Gage slunk along the muddy walkway. Wooden planks had once been placed along the edge of the lane, but they had rotted away and the woody pulp only added to the muck that never seemed to dry out. The cold mud sucked at his worn boots and oozed in through the holes in the thin soles.

The sun was up, but the sky was dark with low hovering clouds of steam and soot. There had been no wind for days now. The still air had allowed the smog to settle in and make itself at home, hugging up against the buildings so the sun's rays barely managed to cut through and lift the shadows from between the structures. He reached up to tighten his filter mask, once more cursing the luck that lost him his goods and his breather, such as it was, to boot.

Normally, he'd be holed up somewhere tight and hopefully dry, but because of the time he'd spent battling with Clax before they had finally made their truce, he'd missed his chance to climb unseen into the Nest, or any of the gang's other rooftop sleeping spots. Asides, he didn't want to have to explain to Checks that he had no shares to offer. And he likely wouldn't for some time. Not after losing his loot. The loss of the silver chain was an extra gut punch. On top of all that, he wasn't sure how to explain his pact with Clax. Checks would for certain see the trade value of the...device?...creature?...Gage still wasn't quite sure what Clax was. *Not really one thing or the other.*

He lifted the front edge of his jacket and peeked into his shirt pocket where Clax had tucked itself up in order to stay hidden. Must be nice to be dry and warm like that. Not that a bit of metal and clockworks needed to stay warm. Dry was another thing. He wondered again what made Clax work. Sure, the clockwork winding key that folded in between its wings looked just like the ones he'd seen on the wind-up toys in the shop windows around Landings during the time nearest St. Nick's Night. But those things didn't act like they had minds of their own. And they didn't fly, neither. Not so's he knew. He had no idea if they could make a dust that stank of storms and burning things, and sizzled when mixed with blood, but he doubted it. No. There was more to Clax than cogs and wheels. Had to be.

His stomach rumbled and he sighed. Must be nice not to have to worry about eating, either. He'd tried going by St. Petra's, hoping to see Nobs and maybe pick up a stale crust. Only the caretaker had shooed him away and told him to come back later. Fussing about boys who disappeared when you needed them most as he swept the messy yard of the previous evening's crumbs.

"You talking 'bout Nobs?" Gage had asked, hovering at the yard's rusted gate.

"Ah dursn't know what him's name be, just that

him's naught but skin an' bones, and gots a bad habit of scrubbing at him's filthy nose. And aren't worth his feed if he dursn't show up to do him's work." The cantankerous man had glared at Gage.

Gage had backed away from the yard, his head pounding. Wasn't like Nobs to miss out on St. Petra's. Had Cutter nabbed him? Why hadn't Gage stayed around to make sure his mate had gotten away 'stead of heading off to Tinker's like it was the most important thing? What was wrong with him that he could let something like that happen to one of his own mates, his spit-sworn family? Why was it he was always out doing something else when someone needed him?

He let the front of his jacket fall back into place and glanced around to certain himself no one had noticed. Wouldn't do to give nobody ideas that he was hiding anything of worth on his person. Not where he was headed.

Despite Checks's warnings against it, he was more determined than ever to find his missing mates. And now, especially, Nobs, who had always been the kindest among them.

Cutter had said something last night about sending them all "to the pits," but Gage had no idea what that meant. There weren't any pits that he knew of in Landings. Though, a fair number of folks might think the whole place one big reeking one. That meant he'd have to find out what Cutter was up to. And to do that, he needed information. Since he couldn't get it from Tinker, the blasted old thief, he'd have to go to the old Whisper woman. And to do that, he'd have to do something truly dangerous—cross into Dartlings territory.

***

By the time Gage reached the edge of Lostuns territory, the workday had come on of a sudden. The busy roadway was filled with the hustle and jostle of all manner of movers, from work wagons to handcarts and even a few fine steamer carriages. All of them carrying goods and people betwixt one end of the city and the 'nother.

He glanced across the wide thoroughfare that marked the boundary of Dartlings' turf and swallowed hard.

The last time he'd been here, they'd been on a rumble to keep the Dartlings from traipse-passing on Lostuns' land. Gage's crew had managed to hold their own and make a point, but it had been a bad day for both sides, filled with cuts and breaks and bruises that festered and healed slow and painful.

Maybe this wasn't such a good idea, after all. Maybe he could still find a way to convince Tinker to help. But, naw. Even if the crooked old ruster wasn't responsible for the theft of Gage's stash, there was no time to get more loot. Asides, he'd made a sworn oath to Clax not to turn it over. So, really, he had nothing of value, 'cept the old pocket watch still in his safe stash. But that had been the only thing his Mam had of his pap's, aside from the silver chain what was now long gone. Why the cracked tarnished watch seemed to matter so much more'n the chain, he couldn't right figure, but for some reason he couldn't bring himself to part with that last family trinket.

With no other options, it was seek out the Whisperer and hope the old woman might be in a sharing mood, or head back to the Nest, empty handed. And forget about his mates. Including Nobs.

Nawp. He'd set this course and he'd follow it. No matter what. Mates was family. And family was everything.

Fighting against the tightness that gripped his ribs, he dragged in a deep breath, ducked his head and skittered across the busy street. Being out and visible during the morning like this made his skin itch. He, along with the rest of the Lostuns, always did their best picking and creeping during shift changes when tired workers were less likely to notice a small boy's hand reaching into a sack or a pocket amidst the crush.

While it would be a dangerous undertaking at any time, his best bet of getting across Dartlings' turf was to pass unnoticed. Crossing during the early hours and mixing with the normal bustle of traffic meant walking outside his home territory in full daylight. Keeping to the most crowded places would be both more dangerous and safer. Dangerous because he was more visible and could be potentially called out as a loiterer, or worse, an orphan. Safer because as long as he stayed to himself and kept moving, he was unlikely to be spotted by a rival gang member.

He hoped.

Sticking to the inside of the walkways where he could duck in and out of doorways and alleys, he dodged surly workers carrying their mid-shift meals and jigged around house servants out running errands for their employers. Most folks of any real means spent their outings walking the greenways or dining in the fancy coffee houses and restaurants in the finer parts of town. Yet, as raggedy as he was, Gage stood out among the workaday foot traffic this time of day. So, he kept his head down, watching for and expecting danger at every turn.

He'd just reached the midway point to his destination when a buzzing erupted from inside his shirt pocket that made him jump sideways and bump into a burly worker who shoved him off with an angry grunt. "Sorry," he muttered.

The man sneered and resumed his heavy gait.

As Gage scurried away, something poked him in the ribs. "Stay still," he told Clax, setting a hand against his jacket where it hid inside his shirt. "This hain't a pleasure fair out here."

Clax buzzed back at him, sending a warm tickling sensation across his chest.

Just then, something sharp poked into his back and he stiffened, preparing to dodge into the crowd.

"Keep walking up to the alley, nice and calm like, then turn in," a voice hissed into his ear before he could move.

That voice. He knew that voice. Ding-dangit. Not just any Dartling had caught him up, but it had to be HER. Wynd. Leader of the Dartlings, and down-and-dirty, can't-be-trusted pact breaker. "And why would I do that?" His brain did whirly-gigs trying to figure a way out.

He couldn't just walk into an alley with her. She'd be bound to have her crew waiting to pounce. They'd wreck him. Worse, they'd be bound to pick him over after, and when they did, they'd find Clax. No way was that going to happen.

"Elsewise, I'll stick you, and you won't go any farther."

"Here?" he asked. "With all these people as could witness the crime?" If he didn't do what she said, might she really stick him?

"Crime? What crime? An orphan thief that stumbled into a strange part of town to bleed? And even if they did see, who would blame me? A sweet young thing that just happened to be nearby when the foul death-bringer came trotting along for his due?"

"Sweet, young thing? You?" Gage snorted.

She pressed the sharp point of her weapon harder into his back. "Don't get smart. And don't flatter yourself thinking anyone will care if something happens to you." Her tone grew into an angry snarl. "You're on *our* turf, now. And you'd best do as I say."

Gage stopped in his tracks. *Ding-dangit!* He should have had a weapon handy. But his small notched pocketknife was tucked away. Asides, it was small and dull and it'd be no use in an actual fight. "Might as well stick me, then. Not like you hain't done such nasty things afore."

"Your gang broke the rules first." Wynd poked him in the back.

Gage jerked forward at the sharp jab. "That's a dirty lie."

"Deny it all you want." Wynd continued to poke him, nudging him slowly forward. "Checks drew first edge and first blood."

Gage's face grew hot. No way Checks would do something so foul. He was tough on their crew, but he'd not endanger them like that. And then go and lie about it? Naw. The rumble terms had been agreed to and oathed on. Spit and all. Checks wouldn't risk their mates by going back on an oath. "Your side brought the cutters," he grumbled. "Lostuns fight fair."

"Not going to argue with a liar." Wynd gave him another poke.

The alley loomed up ahead and the spit in Gage's mouth dried to dust, but he tucked his shaking hands inside his sleeves. The Dartlings weren't known for their softness, and everyone knew their leader was the hardest of them all, but he'd be rusted if he'd let her see fear on him. He jumped when Clax buzzed against his chest once more. He wanted to tell Clax to flee, but he didn't want to let his captor know what prize hid tucked inside his pocket. He chewed his bottom lip, trying to form a plan. But he'd always been more about acting than planning. Checks did the Lostuns' planning. Another reason he was their leader, and Gage wasn't.

As they neared the alley, an idea lit up his brain. If he tripped and fell before the turn, he might be able to dive below knifepoint and scarper off before her gang caught him up. Then he'd not need to give away the presence of Clax. He could keep his word to help protect the clockwork fairy and maybe, just maybe, still get to the Whisperer and find out what she knew.

But the sharp poker jabbed harder into his back followed by the words, "Don't even think about it."

"Wait up," Gage said, turning his head to look over his shoulder in sudden realization. "That hain't a knife."

Her eyes grew wide in her narrow face and for a moment he thought he saw fear, but then she jabbed him again. "Don't need a knife for the likes of you." She held up the sharpened stick tight in her fist, then dodged to one side and gave him a hard shove.

The alley he fell into wasn't much more than a narrow space between two filthy, muck-covered brick buildings. It was filled with piles of cast-off parts and garbage and smelled of rotted food and rodent droppings, along with some other things Gage preferred not to think about. But the one thing that was missing was Dartlings. There wasn't a hide nor hair of any gang members other than *her*. Their rotted leader.

"So, it's just you, Wynd-double-dealing-Dartling." Gage picked himself up and turned to face her.

"Well, if it isn't Gage-lying-liar-Lostun. Surprised to see you wandering so far from home." She stood in the opening of the narrow space, legs spread wide, blocking him in. "You looking for another beating? Where's *your* gang of rotters, then?"

The stick in her hand looked even sharper than it

had felt when it was poked into his back, but Gage stood his ground. "Don't think there's going to be any beatings. You're as alone as I am."

"Don't need anyone else." She waved the pointy stick in his direction. "And I'm in full rights with you trespassing on Dartlings turf."

Gage held up his hands. "Just passing through."

Her eyes narrowed. "To where?"

Gage ground his teeth. *Shut up*, he told himself. *Never give up anything you needn't*, Checks would've cuffed him. He scrunched up his face. "Just heading over to the docks for a quick bit o' business."

"Like I'm supposed to believe that." She sneered. "Everyone knows Dockers don't do business with raggedy orphans."

"Believe what you want," Gage huffed.

She shoved the stick in his face, the pointy end not more than an inch from his left eye. "Tell me where you're really going, or I *will* stick you."

"You might as well go ahead. You're planning to anyway. Just like a lousy Dartling to come after an unarmed person with a weapon."

"Take that back," Wynd hissed.

"Why should I?"

Across the way on the far side of the lane, a figure stopped and made an abrupt turn in their direction. Gage jerked his head over Wynd's shoulder. "Might want to look behind you."

She tensed, then let out a small laugh. "Nice try. Not falling for it."

"Not. A. Trick," Gage said, as he watched the figure head across the street.

"Right." Wynd twirled the stick in her hand.

"Oy, careful, get out of the street," someone yelled.

"Police bizness. Keep to yerself," yelled Cutter, as he dodged a cart.

Wynd's face grew pale. "Crooked Cutter?" she

whispered.

"Yeah," Gage said. "We need to skitter. Now."

But Wynd was already running, her tangled hair blowing behind her as her long limbs propelled her down the lane and around a corner.

Gage froze. He needed to skeet-daddle. Cutter had got 'round the snarl of traffic and was storming toward the alley. But with no clear idea of where to go in rival territory, Gage had no option except to follow Wynd.

Chapter Sixteen
In a Pickle

A few turns and a short run later, Wynd leaped over a stack of barrels sitting in front of the large gray loading door of Varney's Vinegars. Gage leaped in behind her and dropped down into the narrow space between the closed door and the barrels.

"What d'you think you're doing?" Wynd whisper-growled beside him. She raised her sharp stick between them. It wasn't much, but it was all she had.

"No beefs." Gage pushed out his words between panting breaths. "Least not till we know we're out of Cutter's way." He spit into his palm and held his hand out to her.

Wynd tightened her grip on her pointed stick and shook her head. She opened her mouth to say something else, when they heard the tread of heavy boots and ragged gasps.

They tucked down tight behind the stack of leaky sour barrels. Wynd kept her eyes pasted on Gage.

She squatted there all tensed up, feeling like a cat ready to pounce on a pigeon. Only, it was more like she'd be the pigeon if she turned her back on a dab-rusted Lostun. All her bones and muscles quivered and her insides grew tight.

The space between the barrels and the sides of the building's doorway arches wasn't enough for an adult to get through, but what if Cutter decided to try and move the front barrels? They'd find themselves trapped between the warehouse doors and an angry copper. So, she clamped her mouth shut against all the ugly things she wanted to spew at Gage.

Gage tried not to show his fear, but Wynd could see it on him, all tensed up and practically shivering with it. She thought of Micah and Jasp and those first nights out on the streets, begging and hiding, just trying to stay alive. And together. She gulped down the pain that tried to escape.

Heavy footsteps clomped nearer, along with loud and raspy breaths. Sure as sure, it was him, just the other side of the barrels from them.

Wynd squinched her eyes shut and stayed as still as stone.

A beefy hand slapped at the barrels and Cutter let out an ugly curse. "You're slowing down, Cutter. Not ever gonna reach that retired-ment, if you can't even catch a couple a rot-dodgered orphants." He drew in a jaggedy breath. "'Course, wasn't your fault that dung-ridden steamer cart got in the way. People ought to need a permit to drive in the city." He hocked up a wad of phlegm and spat it out. Then he shuffled about a bit, as if trying to see around the barrels. Finally, he moved off, still muttering. "You got a contract to fulfill. Quotas to meet and all like that."

A long time passed before Wynd opened her eyes and then it was only to glare at Gage. "What's with following me?" She kept her voice quiet, which only made her anger more pronounced.

"Where else was I going to go?" Gage whispered back. "Not like I know Dartlings' turf, nor where to hole up."

"You'd not be welcome in a Dartlings' bolt-hole, no matter."

"Well, not unless I'm along with the gang's leader." Gage gave her a foolish smile.

"I'm not—" Wynd clamped her teeth down.

"Not what?" Gage asked.

"Not inviting you in." Wynd waved her pointy stick at him. "So, you need to scarper on back to where you come from."

"Can't." Gage leaned back against the heavy warehouse doors. "Got business to attend."

Wynd leaned forward, eyes narrowed. "Business? In Dartlings' territory? What kind of business?"

Gage sighed. "If I tell you, will you allow me passage there and back?"

"Maybe." Wynd screwed up her face in thought. "But only if your business isn't the funny kind."

"I need to talk to the Whisperer," Gage blurted.

Wynd heard the name like a slap. "What about?"

He stared at her like he knew what she was thinking, but she'd already had enough fortune telling to last her a lifetime. "Might as well spill it," she told him. "You've already been caught on another gang's turf. Might make a difference to fess up why. Might be the only thing that does." She waved the stick at him meaningfully.

"I'm looking for someone."

"Not good enough."

"Fine. We got mates missing and I figger she might know how to find 'em." Gage slumped. "Satisfied?"

"Nope." Wynd shook her head.

"What d'ya mean, nope?" Gage pulled his jacket

tighter around his body. "Thought you said you'd give me safe passage, if I told you my business, and I have."

Wynd eyed him closer, wondering if he was up to something, but he kept his hands where they were. "Didn't say I'd grant passage. Only said, 'maybe.'"

Gage opened his mouth to speak, but she cut him off. "Didn't say I wouldn't grant passage, neither."

"Then what *are* you saying?" Gage asked, his mouth drawn down into a frown.

"Talking to Whisperer won't do you any good," Wynd mumbled.

"How the cogs would you know?"

"Because..." Wynd looked him hard in the eye. She thought about what the Whisperer had said about them being 'across the water.' Wondered if she should tell Gage the whole of it. But why should she share what she knew with a Lostun? "I already asked about...the missing...streeters." She looked away so he couldn't see the half-lie on her face. "And she's either not knowing or not telling."

"What d'you mean, you already asked?"

Wynd poked at a barrel stave with her stick. "We got mates gone missing, too." She thought about Micah and Jasp. Both her brothers had disappeared at the same time. Again. And she'd let it happen. Again. How could she? She wasn't only their sister, she was their leader. Or had been. She glanced up at Gage. This was probably not the best time to mention to him that she couldn't grant passage, even if she wanted to. Not since she'd stepped down from leading the Dartlings. Not since she was on her own, searching for Micah and Jasp. And just about as much an outsider here as Gage.

Gage sagged back against the doors, a look of sadness filling his face. "Now what?" he asked. "What in the ding-dang rusted works can we do?"

"We?" Wynd was startled by the emotion that surged in her heart at the thought of having help to find her brothers. Losing Micah and Jasp had been hard. Losing the Dartlings gang's support had been an added burden. Being alone…that was the hardest thing of all. She tensed her muscles and forced the annoying tears that pushed at the corners of her eyes to go back where they'd come from. Crying never fixed anything. Living on the street these past few years had taught her that. The hopefulness that had risen in her chest, too, she pushed away. That was a leftover from the before life. Not something that belonged here and now. No. Hope had no place in this. Only the fierce belief that she would find Micah and Jasp and keep them safe the way she'd promised she would.

"What's wrong with 'we'?" Gage asked.

Wynd narrowed her eyes at him. "Why come looking for the Whisperer? Don't you Lostuns have your own sources?"

Gage swallowed hard. "My source weren't for giving out anything…useful."

"Then what's the point of working together?" Wynd tried to sound firm, but she felt herself wavering. It would be good to have help, but how could she trust a Lostun?

"I said my source weren't in a giving mood, not that I didn't know anything."

"What?" Wynd blurted. "What do you know?"

"I think you know something. And since I know something, too, if we share what we know, we both know more. Maybe that way we can figure out a way to find our mates and help them." He gave her a hopeful look.

"You think they're in danger, same as me," Wynd murmured.

"Any of your mates ever run off before?"

Anger smacked into Wynd of a sudden. She shook her head no and pointed her sharp stick at him. "They wouldn't do that." Her words came out as a growl, but there was an underlying doubt that she hated hearing in her own voice. *Believe. Believe. Believe.* She forced herself to repeat the word over and over in her head.

"Not saying they would," Gage said, calmly. "Just a question."

Wynd put her stick away. "They're not just my mates," she told him. "They're..."

"I know," Gage said in a gentle voice. "They're family."

"How'd you know that?" Wynd asked in surprise.

"Hain't they all? Family, that is? All the family we got in the world is our mates." Something mournful crossed his face when he said it.

Wynd grew thoughtful but didn't say anything. She understood what he meant, though she wanted to point out that Micah and Jasp really were family. Only, she could tell by the way he said those words, Gage's ties to his own mates was, in its way, as strong a bond as hers by blood.

"Fine," she finally said. "Not that it means much, but Whisperer told me they're across some water. But that could mean anything."

"Yeah. Maybe." Gage scratched his cheek. "But it's something."

"So?"

"So, what?"

"So, I told you what I know..."

Gage frowned. "All I know is, whatever is going on has some people spooked-like."

"Then they *are* in danger."

"Hain't we all?"

They grew quiet, listening to the sounds of passing carts and people. The clop-clop-clop of horses' hooves and chug-chug-chug of steam haulers wrapped over and around the tramping steps of passing feet. After a while, the sounds lessened and the sky grew dimmer.

"Time to go." Wynd stood up and raised herself up high enough to see over the tops of the barrels.

"Go where?" Gage asked, standing beside her and looking out on the street.

"Away from here, for one thing."

"But we hadn't made a pact." His eyes grew wide.

"No time for that." She clambered up to the top of the barrels and nodded over her shoulder just as the warehouse doors behind them swung inward.

"Oy, you rabble best scat!" A short man hollered when he caught sight of them. "Lessen you wants the law called."

Wynd waved at the warehouser, who squinted an eye at her. Then she signaled for Gage to follow her and dropped down on the street side of the barrels.

Gage scrabbled over the top of the pile and leaped to the street behind her, and the two of them skittered off down the lane.

Chapter Seventeen
Temper, Temper

Gage followed in Wynd's wake, glancing over his shoulder at every turn. They'd no pact betwixt them. And for all he knew, she was leading him into a trap. But he had few options at this point. Her route twisted and turned, heading up lanes and cutting across alleys. At one point they ducked into a rundown tea house and slipped through the kitchen and out the back door, with nary a glance from the tea drinkers nor servers, which made Gage feel nigh invisible. There were no such shortcuts in Lostuns territory. Every bolt-hole and hidey had been hard won and not a single shop owner turned a blind eye to traipse-passers without payment. Tinker was the perfect example. No matter what Gage did, he always sunk deeper and deeper into debt.

After gobs of running and loads of turns, they finally reached an old ramshackle building that looked to be deserted. Wynd slipped around the corner and clambered up a stack of debris, pushed open a smudge-covered window and disappeared into a dark space. Gage stood in the narrow alley, staring up at the window.

Clax buzzed inside his pocket as he waited, swiveling his head from side to side, certain that this would be his undoing. "Shhhh," he said. "Just a bit—"

Wynd stuck her head out and hissed at him. "Safer in here."

Gage shrugged off the nerves that skittered over his body and climbed up to the window. He peered into the dark, searching for signs of a trap, or the shadowy outlines that would reveal a crowd of Dartlings ready to do him foul, but the place looked empty. After a moment, he slipped through into the darkened building.

"Come on," Wynd told him, waving a hand as she jogged across the empty floor toward a far corner filled with deep shadows.

He shook his head, thinking how easy it would be for her gang to jump him and leave his battered remains for Constable Cutter or the like. "Not till I have a pact."

"That can wait," she urged.

Clax buzzed a warning in his pocket, but he gave it a small pat that felt more confident than it probably should. Wynd hadn't done him foul, yet. And she seemed to want to find her missing mates as much as he did his. He swallowed his concern and followed after her.

Finally, they reached the back corner of the building and Wynd turned to him and spun around with a flourish. "Welcome to our humble establishment. We will be retiring early, due to a shortage of, um, well, pretty much everything. However, feel free to tuck into a nice empty crate for a bit of a sleep. There is no need to worry about the local constabulary discovering our whereabouts. That is, as long as we have moved on prior to the next big shipment of special goods."

"Special goods, is it? Oh, that's just grand. Out of the firebox and into the boiler." Gage gave the space the once over. "Don't you ever wonder, though?

"About what?" she asked.

"Why so much space is devoted to smuggling. Doesn't anyone make a living from honest trade?"

"I don't truly know. Besides, who are we to talk?" Wynd let out a laugh that made Gage chuckle.

In his pocket, Clax buzzed in annoyance. He patted at his chest to calm his mechanical ally, but that only made Clax buzz harder. It stretched up and pushed aside his jacket to peer out.

"What's that sticking out from your pocket?" Wynd asked. Her face filled with sudden suspicion.

"Don't know what you're talking of." Gage pulled at his jacket so it covered his pocket and shrugged.

"Don't be playing games with me." Wynd's eyes narrowed. She grabbed a pair of thick canvas gloves from a shelf, yanked a steam hose off a nearby hook and pointed it directly at Gage's head. "I know sparkles when I see them. Something glittery is in your pocket, and I want to know what it is."

Gage crossed his arms. "So, threats already, is it? And like as not a phony one, I expect. Just like using a pointy little stick for a knife."

"I don't make false threats. That pointy little stick is sharp enough to puncture gizzards. And this"— Wynd pointed the hose at the wall and pulled back the handle till a hot spurt of steam hissed out of the nozzle—"will cook your eyeballs and boil your brains."

A whirring blur zipped from Gage's pocket, flew into the shadows and landed on the top of a stack of empty crates. It glowed a fiery red, buzzing angrily.

"What *is* that?" Wynd asked in wonder, wavering between pointing the steam coupler at Gage or the glowing, glittering thing perched above him.

Clax let out an ugly sound.

"It's none of your bizzy-ness." Gage set his jaw.

Wynd directed the hose up toward the glowing object. "Tell me what it is, or I'll turn it into a puddle."

Clax flashed a deeper red at the same time as Gage said, "Now, you've gone and done it."

Wynd gave him a hard look. "What are you on about?"

"Clax doesn't like to be threatened," he warned.

Wynd eyed the glowing clockwork and pointed the steam hose at it. "I'll do more than threaten, if you don't tell me what it is."

In a flash, Clax leaped into the air and swerved across the space between them before Wynd could blink. "Ow!" She shouted, nearly dropping the hose. "It bit me."

"I tried to tell you." Gage smirked at her. "And it doesn't bite, so much as stab." He made a motion like he was thrusting a sword into an imaginary enemy.

Wynd pointed the hose at Clax and gripped the spigot in her gloved hand. "Let's just see how it likes this."

"No!" Gage dove at her, knocking the hose from her grip as she opened the valve and loosed a jet of hot steam. The power of it knocked over a stack of empty crates. They crashed to the floor in a shatter of splinters. The hose thrashed across the floor still spewing the deadly steam. Gage grabbed Wynd by the arm and dragged her back behind a stack of metal machine parts.

"Let go," she yelled, yanking her arm out of his grasp.

"Fine!" Gage shouted. "Go get your face melted off. See if I care." He looked around the plant, searching frantically for the clockwork fairy. "Clax?" he called out over the hissing steam and the noise of the hose that still slapped the floor, its metal fixtures clanking and clacking against the cobblestones.

Wynd ducked behind the wall of metal gears and fixtures. "How do we stopper it?"

"What do you mean 'we'?" he shot back at her.

"Well," she grumped over the noise of the steam, "we're both here and that"—she pointed at the writhing, clanking hose—"is about as loud an alarm as a watchdog. So, if *we* want to keep from getting caught out in this not-official hidey, *we*"—she waved her hand at the two of them—"need to shut that off. Now."

"So, now you want my help?" Gage asked. "No truce when you held the upper hand, but now...?"

Wynd gave him a dirty look. "Truce." She took off the heavy glove, spit into her right hand and held it out to him, her upper lip curling in distaste.

Gage eyed her dirty hand and tugged at the lock of hair that had fallen across his forehead. Then he spit into his hand and reached for hers.

But before their palms could meet, a red blur whizzed between them. Clax hovered in the air in front of Gage and faced Wynd, tiny sword drawn, wings beating a humming blur. Sharp notes of anger jangled from the clockwork fairy.

Wynd jumped back.

"Come on, Clax," Gage said. "We need her."

The fairy drew a circle in the air with the tip of its sword pointing at Wynd, then pointed at the hose that still snaked across the floor. Clouds of steam rose into the air and filled the space.

"Oh, pardon me." Wynd's tone was mocking, but her eyes stayed on Clax. "But you drew first blood." She touched her ear and held out her bloody fingers.

Clax let out a peal of tinkling that sounded

distinctly like snickering and flashed a lighter shade of red.

"I don't think it likes you," Gage said.

The fairy flashed blue, then glowed red again.

"It definitely doesn't like you." Gage looked down at the cold glob of spit in his hand. "Clax, we need to get across Dartling's turf. And we need out of here before somebody comes to inspect the hubbuballoo. Someone's bound to have heard all that." He pointed at a pile of tumbled containers and the still wriggling steam hose.

"Hullaballoo," Wynd said.

Gage glared at her. "Whatever. We hain't got time to be ins-fightin'. We need a truce."

"Infighting," Wynd corrected under her breath.

Flashing and jingling, Clax backed-up in midair until its feet touched down onto Gage's shoulder, sword still pointed at Wynd.

"I think that means yes to a truce, but any funny business and Clax'll...put out an eye." Gage improvised.

Clax glanced at him and shrugged.

"I already offered a truce," Wynd griped. "And I keep my word, unlike some others I know." She glared at Gage and Clax, but stuck out her hand again.

Gage was about to say something nasty back to her when they heard the distant sound of a copper's whistle. He thrust his hand suddenly into Wynd's, gave it one quick shake, then pulled it back and wiped his palm on his pant leg. "Time to go," he said, reaching for a handhold to pull himself up to the top of the stack of equipment. Wynd shimmied up beside him. He stood atop the heap of metal and looked for a way out that wouldn't take them across the path of the still thrashing steam hose.

"We go there." He pointed to a transom window

across the way that hung partly open. He picked his way to the edge of the pile and crouched ready to spring. Climbing the pile of metal parts had been the easy part. Leaping across the crisscrossing jumble of steam pipes without protection would be trickier. He took in a steadying breath as the copper's whistle grew louder.

"Wait," Wynd said.

"What?" he asked, impatience showing in his voice.

She handed him one of the heavy gloves. "You might need this."

"Thanks." Gage pulled on the glove.

Wynd shrugged. "Truce means allies. Allies help one another."

"Long as the truce holds," Gage said.

"Told ya. *I* keep my word." Wynd's eyes narrowed.

Gage gritted his teeth against the swear that rose up from his gullet. "We need to go." He pointed toward the window. "Now."

Wynd opened her mouth to say something, but just then the main warehouse door slammed open.

Chapter Eighteen
Playing Chicken

It took the better part of a half-hour of Wynd leading him hilter-skilter through the shadows before she paused beside another dark building. As they snaked their way through the darkness, Gage grabbed her by the sleeve and pulled her to a stop beside a broken wooden fence.

"What now?" She whispered.

Gage jerked his chin in the direction of the ragged fence. "There's an opening here."

Wynd should her head. "But that's someone's yard. We can't hide in there."

"I know," Gage said, trying not to sound annoyed. "But look."

Inside the busted up wooden fence was a rickety henhouse.

"I am not stealing a chicken." Wynd shot glances around the darkened space, as if expecting something to jump out at them at any moment. "Too noisy."

"Not them," Gage pointed just beyond the coop to

where a small sack sat atop a pile of odds and ends. "Could be something good in it. Maybe some cracked corn."

"Oh." Wynd licked her lips.

Gage swung a weathered slat sideways, the wood creaking against the rusty nail that held it in place, creating a narrow opening in the fence. "Think you can squeeze in between these two boards?"

Clax buzzed inside his shirt pocket. "No, Clax," he whispered, "this hain't a job for you."

The clockwork's sudden stillness was as pointed as its blade, but he ignored it.

Wynd pursed her lips together and nodded. While Gage held the slats open, she twisted sideways and slid her shoulders through the narrow space. The rough boards scraped against her, catching on the fabric of her frayed jacket with a tearing sound as she pushed her way inside the small yard, and her sleeve caught on a jagged splinter pulling her off balance. She managed to free her sleeve only to stumble and fall into the yard in a heap. Her breath rushed out with a loud oof.

Both she and Gage froze, afraid someone might have heard them. From inside the henhouse came the stir of ruffled feathers and the quiet clucking of a nervous hen resettling itself beneath the rotting leanto that sheltered the chicken coop. Then stillness filled the air. After what seemed like forever, Gage hissed at her and Wynd shook herself loose with a shiver. Across the narrow yard sat the small grain sack. The bulge at the bottom confirmed there was something inside, and Wynd's stomach rumbled at the possibility of food.

She stood up slow and careful, then picked her way around the piles of debris strewn across the space and reached for the bag. Something wriggled inside it and she drew her hand back. A rat the size of both her fists scrambled out of the sack and hissed at her. She let out a yelp.

A dog barked from inside the dark house and someone yelled. Wynd started, grabbed the bag, darted back to the fence, and squeezed through just as the back door opened and lamplight flared from inside the house.

Gage dropped the fence slat and it swung back into place, and the two of them skittered down the dark alleyway. Behind them a voice rang out. "Thieves! I'll set the hound on ya."

But Gage and Wynd had already turned the corner and scrambled off into the dark, fleeing like skittery mice.

Chapter Nineteen
Make-Believe

"You're a liar." Wynd grumbled, holding her hands out to the small flame. "Everyone knows it."

Gage's face burned. His skin buzzed as if he'd been stung by a thousand bees. "Not a liar." He stirred the grain into the steaming water. He tapped the stick on the edge of the can, watching as the porridge thickened. The sack of grain they'd stolen held only a handful of rough cracked wheat. It weren't much of a meal, but boiled in water it would fill their bellies and warm them. "I forget sometimes, is all."

"Oh?" Her voice held a sneer that he could practically feel. "Did you somehow forget that porridge isn't pheasant?"

"I only thought you'd like to play the game. The Lostuns always did."

"Game?" She hurled the question at him. "Your lot makes a game of starving?"

"No!" Gage threw back at her, anger enflaming his blood. At this rate, he wasn't going to need food to warm him. This girl was managing to do that all on her own. "That's not it, at all. It just seemed to always make whatever meager stuff we got go down a bit better if we, you know, pretended."

"Pretended?" Wynd rubbed her hands together, then shoved them under her armpits.

Gage looked away, suddenly embarrassed to be telling her about the game. "We'd pretend the food was special. That we was having roasted duck, or pig with a big red apple stuffed inside its mouth." His voice dropped almost to a whisper. "When Nobs wouldn't eat, we'd get him to pretend the hard bread we'd found was fancy pastries or some of those floofy stoosels."

"You mean streusel?" Wynd's mouth had begun to water at the thought of sweets and cakes.

Clax jangled a warning at them and Gage jumped.

The tin can rattled and the porridge boiled over with a hiss. Gage grabbed the stick and stirred their small meal down. Then, using the gloves they'd managed to hang onto during their escape from the smuggler's warehouse, he lifted the can from the fire and set it to cool in the frigid air. He handed one of the gloves to Wynd.

"So, you were playing a game with me?" Wynd asked, taking the glove and slipping it over one of her hands, then shoving the other one in beside it with a small sigh. "What about all the other stories?"

Gage shrugged and smirked. "Stories is stories. They pass the time when you're all packed in like sardinnias in a hideout, or other times when you're trying to keep warm 'neath a bridge."

"You mean sardines."

"Whatever." Gage licked his fingertip and quickly touched the side of the can to check if it was cool enough yet to pick up. No hiss but still hot to the touch. The cold night air had worked fast, but the porridge still steamed. He picked up the warm can and stirred it a bit, releasing some more of the heat before offering it to Wynd.

She eyed the can for a moment before removing a hand from the heavy glove and taking the porridge from him. "Thank you." She rolled it between her hands, letting the heat soak into her shivery fingers.

She raised the can to her lips and tilted it back enough to allow a glop of mealy porridge to slide into her mouth. She closed her eyes and tried to pretend, but the porridge tasted like what it was, porridge that had been made with old stale wheat that had been destined for someone's chickens until she and Gage had come along.

Gage swallowed hard, his jaw tight. His deep hunger sat on his face the way it often had on Jasp's and Micah's. And yet he had offered her first slurps.

"Mmmmm," she said after forcing herself to swallow the lumpy mass. "That is perhaps the best roast venison I have ever tasted." She offered the can to Gage.

Gage started, hand extended to take the food, and a small smile tugged at the corners of his mouth. "It's always best with the extra seasoning."

He took a mouthful of the porridge and swallowed, letting the warmth of the meager food slide down into his cold empty belly, before passing the can back to Wynd. "The beef shank hain't half bad, neither. Try some?"

"Don't mind if I do." There only a few mouthfuls of porridge for each of them, but when they'd finished, not only had the food and fire warmed them, but the chill that had been a wall between them seemed to have melted just a wee bit, as well.

Wynd gazed on as the clockwork fairy buzzed around Gage's head, making those jingling noises that sounded more and more like words. After a few minutes, Clax landed on Gage's knee facing Wynd. Gage reached out a hand, unfolded a tiny key from the middle of the fairy's back and gave it a few turns.

"Clax don't eat," he told Wynd. "But it needs to be—ow!" He yanked his hand away from the fairy, who now stood facing him, sword in hand. "What was that for?" He stuck his bloody finger in his mouth.

The fairy jingled and jangled its discordant notes, then leaped into the air and flew off.

Wynd smirked at him. "Your little pet bites the hand that feeds—ouch!" Her hand flew to her head where the angry pixie had ripped out several hairs and hovered over her, dangling them in a huff.

It was Gage's turn to smirk. "Clax does have a mind of its own."

Clax dropped the hairs, letting them float to the floor one by one.

"Hmm, Clax don't like you much." He shrugged and beckoned the creature over to him. Clax buzzed around him a few times, then settled back onto his knee and allowed him to turn the key in its back a few more times. Clax glared at Wynd the entire time, with crossed arms, as if daring her to do anything other than sit and watch.

As soon as Gage finished turning the key, the fairy leaped into the air, turning a spiral, then looped overhead and disappeared up into the darkness.

They sat in silence until Gage cleared his throat and asked, "How did you end up with the Dartlings?"

Wynd stiffened and eyed him warily before answering. "What's that got to do with anything?"

"Just wondering," Gage tugged at the knotted laces on his scuffed boots. "Making chit-chat to pass the time, is all."

"It's not a happy story for passing time," she said bitterly, hunching over and pulling her thin coat tighter around her.

Gage suddenly noticed how thin her wrists and hands were. He should have given her a larger portion of the food, he thought guiltily, then thought better of it. She was a proud girl. Proud as any he'd ever met, he reckoned, and wouldn't have cared much for his charity.

"Not many are," he said. "I've heard some of the worst, in fact." He thought back to the Lostuns nice safe tuckaways and the nights they'd shared, spilling out their own miserable stories. None of them were happy tales. "Never mind." He pulled his cap down over his eyes and scooted back against the barrels stacked beside them.

Wynd frowned, then bit her lower lip in thought. "What if I told you a story about something else?"

"Like what?" asked Gage, his eyelids half shut.

"What about a 'Once upon a time' story?"

Gage opened one eye to look at her and see if she was teasing him. "Bit old for that, amn't I?"

"I don't know. Someone once told me we're never too old for a good old-fashioned tale. Especially one that brings a bit of adventure in."

"Get plenty of adventure running from old Cutter," Gage mumbled.

"Fine," Wynd huffed. "It's no shine off my apple if you'd rather not."

Gage sat up at her hurt tone. "Go on, then," he said. "Tell me an adventure, but leave out any romancy."

Wynd rolled her eyes. "No romance in my stories. What kind of frilly girl do you take me for?" She spread her arms wide.

"Sorry. Sorry." Gage was beginning to wonder if their truce was worth it. Seemed like he spent all his time trying to be nice to her and she hated every bit of it. "Just, spill it, then."

"Spill it? Hmmmph. You don't spill a good story."

She leaned forward as if passing him a huge secret. "You share it out. Like slices of warm pumpkin pie on a holiday." She licked her lips and Gage's mouth watered.

Wynd shifted to sit cross legged. The hems of her threadbare pants barely reached to her thin ankles, but the cold suddenly didn't seem to bother her as she settled in and began a tale of brave and kindly people, who wore paint on their faces and feathers in their hair and whose most favored daughter, the Princess Dawn Light, was kidnapped by a ship full of fierce pirates.

The story drew Gage in. With his eyes half closed, he could almost see the images dance before him like the moving pictures in the penny halls.

"And then," Wynd said, "when all seemed lost, the princess looked up to see a brave young man standing on the ship's rail crowing like a rooster and calling out to the evil pirate captain. 'Ahoy, ya black-hearted scupper. I challenge you to an honorable duel.'"

Gage opened his eyes. "Pirates hain't honorable."

"Shhhh." Wynd glared at him. "I'm just getting to the best part." She lowered her voice back into her storyteller tone. "The princess looked up at the handsome young man and saw how intense his eyes were and—"

Gage sat up. "Whoa, you said there weren't romancy bits in it."

Wynd blushed, but shook her head. "It's not a romance," she said. "The princess was just going to ask him what his name was. Um, and how he got onto the ship. That's all."

"Oh. Well, then, keep going." Gage leaned back against the barrels.

"Anyway," Wynd continued, with somewhat less enthusiasm, "the princess pointed over to the weapons rack and held up her empty hands to the boy. A look passed between them and, right away, he understood exactly what she wanted even without any words.

"He grabbed up a spare blade and jumped down onto the deck and cut the ropes and then he...he handed her the sword and together they fought all the pirates and made them walk the plank before sailing off across the sea together."

"For treasure?"

"What?" Wynd pushed her tangled hair behind her ear.

"You said they sailed off to cross the sea. Was it treasure they sailed off in search for?"

Clax tinkled in the rafter overhead, and Wynd glared up into the darkness. "Oh. Sure." She searched around her for a comfortable place to curl up for the night. Their tiny fire had gone out and the space had filled with the night's chill air.

"We better sit closer," Gage said suddenly, huffing out a small puff of air and watching the white cloud his breath formed.

"What?" Wynd stared across the dark space in surprise.

"Huddle. You know. To keep warm. Don't your gang ever huddle?"

"Oh, yes. Of course." Wynd crawled forward on her hands and knees until she was beside him.

"Better already, en't it?" Gage shifted closer to her, then sat back up. "Oy. I think if maybe we push some of these barrels into more of a circle that'll help even more." He stood up and grabbed the top rim of one of the wooden barrels. "Ooof. Lend a hand, will ya?"

Wynd leaped to her feet and gripped the top of the barrel. Together they tipped it on edge and rolled it into place. They did the same with several more containers, then slipped through the space they'd left between two of the heavy barrels.

"There, now," Gage said in satisfaction. "A snug little house for the night."

"If you say so." Wynd let out a shivery yawn.

"Trust me. It'll be warmer than out in the open." Gage settled down onto the floor.

"You've slept in here before?" She sat down beside him.

"Not here." Gage's voice faded into a low whisper. "But plenty of places like it."

Chapter Twenty
Worst-Laid Plans

They woke before dawn and shimmied out of their hidey before the first shift whistle sounded. Once more out in the cold, Wynd shivered.

"What now?" Gage peered around them.

"Well, you heard Cutter talk about pits, right?"

"Yeah." Gage pulled his ragged collar up and hunched his shoulders.

Clax was tucked once more into his pocket at Wynd's suggestion. "So as not to draw attention," she'd told him. But really, she didn't want to give the nasty thing an opportunity to stab her with that ugly needle sword.

Wynd licked her lips. "And I know they're over the water." The thought still made her hands and face feel numb the way they had when the charity workers had come to tell them of her father's shipwreck. She'd let Gage in on that bit of information after they'd made their pact.

"So, that means—"

"Dockers' turf."

"Thought you already checked there?" Gage sounded hopeful.

"I did, but..." She chewed her lower lip in thought. She needed to find Micah and Jasp. Sooner rather than later. But she'd learned on the streets that impatience only gained trouble. And her last visit to Dockers' turf had nearly been her last.

"But what?"

"There was something fishy going on. I just couldn't figure out what, exactly." She didn't mention the threat she'd overheard about Yoahn the Waster not being the worst thing on the sea. Or the odd metal monster. Like as not, a creature like that would have traveled on by now, right? She glanced at Gage's pocket in worry.

Gage rolled his eyes. "There's always something *fishy* going on over there."

"Yeah, well, I mean *extra* fishy swimming in fish sauce," she shot back.

Gage groaned. "Seems like we'd be able to find another way."

"Fine," Wynd groused, "we could always just let Cutter catch us and take us wherever it is this pit is. Then again, we don't know if it's connected to the bit about over the water. So, we might just end up in a hole somewhere."

"All right. You made your point." Gage rubbed his hands over his face. "But Dockers. They're worse than..."

"Worse than what?" Wynd gave him her most evil-eyed look.

Gage shrugged.

"No. Go ahead, tell me. Who are the Dockers worse than?"

"Pretty much any other gang?" Gage looked sheepish.

"Right." Wynd shook her head at him. "I'm sure that's what you meant to say in the first place." She started off toward the docks.

"Wait." Gage hurried after her. "I got another idea."

"*You* have an *idea*?" She stopped, turned and folded her arms. "Well, let's hear this great plan of yours."

Gage frowned. "I just think it might be worth it after all to find Cutter and see what he knows."

"Find Cutter?!?" Wynd dropped her arms. "And I suppose we just wander up to him on the street and ask him ever so nice what he knows about some missing street urchins? And mayhap we can all go for tea and cakes after."

Gage rolled his eyes again. "No. 'Course not."

"Then what are you suggesting?"

"We follow him."

"What'll be the good of that?" She rubbed her hands together against the damp cold.

"He knows something," Gage insisted. "I know it as well as I know my own name. And if it turns out he hain't connected to the 'cross the water bit' we can still hit Dockers turf. Preferable under full dark, rather than graylight, anyhow."

He was right. The best time to hit Dockers turf was night. "Why don't they just kipper up and sleep during the early graylight like most?"

"Some of them does." Gage shifted his weight from one foot to the other. Clax jingled annoyance from inside his jacket and he stilled. "But they sure got airs. Thinks they're above us all, 'cause they're mostly older. And bigger." He rubbed the side of his face as if recalling an old hurt. "Anyway, they think as they're all a bunch of seafarers, standing their watches, day and night, just like aboard ships. Though, at night, they like to keep tucked up warm, like as with anyone else. "

Wynd knew he was right. She wanted ask how he knew so much about the Dockers, but his eyes had gone twitchy and he refused to look at her. Whatever it was he wasn't going to tell her. But he sure was afraid of the Dockers. Worse than she was. "Fine." It wasn't that it sounded like a good plan to chase the copper who was always chasing them. But they would also need every edge to duck and hide and not get caught on Dockers' turf. So, they had the whole day before they could head that way. And no place to kipper up themselves, since she was no longer welcome in a Dartlings' bolt-hole.

Then again, they'd need all that edge and more not to get caught by Cutter.

Chapter Twenty-One
Dirty Business

It took them most of the day to find Cutter. Seemed the old rotter slept away his mornings in some comfy warm bed. "Figures. Always around when you don't want him. But when you go looking for him..." Gage grumbled.

By the time they caught sight of him sauntering out onto the street, it was well after midday. He first made his way to a nearby coffee house. He stayed inside a long while.

"Probbly having a warm plate of chops and eggs," Gage grumbled, along with his empty belly.

Wynd closed her eyes and sighed. "And a sugary cup of hot tea and milk, I'll bet."

They'd managed to nip a single meat pie off a pie man's cart just after first light. It wasn't much to share between them, but more than nothing. Only that had been hours ago.

The smells that wafted out of the coffee house made their bellies rumble but now that they'd found

Cutter, they couldn't risk another nab. Not if they wanted to remain the pursuers rather than becoming the pursued.

Finally, Cutter emerged, looked both ways up and down the street, then lumbered off. They followed from as close as they could without being seen, which shouldn't have been hard midst the hustle and bustle of the midday traffic. But two raggedy urchins were not altogether invisible. So, they kept their heads down and their eyes up and tried to look as innocent and harmless as possible. All the while, tailing Cutter from one establishment to the next.

Each place the old rotter would enter, be it a butchery or a baker's shop, he tarried for only a few moments before emerging back out onto the street, his hand kneading his jacket pocket as he glanced about warily before moving on.

"Knew he was on the take," Gage said while they loitered outside the tobacconist's to wait as Cutter entered a barber shop across the way.

"Everyone knows." Wynd pushed her tangled hair back behind her ears. "Only nobody cares. Just like nobody cares about us."

"Yeah," Gage agreed, "excepting us."

"Oy, you two. Scoot!" The tobacco seller stepped outside his doorway to shoo them off. "Don't need no funny business round here."

"Wasn't doing nothing," Gage shot back.

"Hah! And me mam wears a red frock coat and rides a fine horse." The balding merchant stood in the doorway and glared. "Won't have the likes of you scaring off my patrons."

"Pah," Gage said. "Not like we hain't got enuff smoke in the air already."

"Get off," growled the man, his whole head turning red. "Or I'll sic the coppers on ya. I can promise ya Cutter's about somewhere." He glowered at them.

"Let's skitter." Wynd grabbed Gage by the arm before he could say anything else. She jerked her chin in the direction of the barber shop, where Cutter was stepping out onto the lane. They ducked around the corner and down a narrow alley.

"Now, you've done it," Wynd scolded. "What if he saw us?

"Aw, he's got bigger business on that street than we'd be." Gage kicked at a pile of rubbish.

"But if he saw us, he might realize we were watching him. Then the whole rest of the day would have been for nothing."

"It hain't us he were looking out for, Wynd. 'Twas other coppers. Or maybe some of them underclothes defectives what sneak about looking for criminals."

"Do you mean plainclothes detectives?"

Muffled laughter came from Clax.

"Whatever."

Wynd huffed out her breath in annoyance. "What if we've lost him?"

"Well, standing around here arguing about what kind of coppers there is hain't helping now, is it?"

From inside his pocket, Clax buzzed to be let out.

"What's it want?" Wynd asked, as Gage opened his coat and Clax zipped out to land on his shoulder.

"I think *Clax* wants to help."

"How—"

Clax leaped into the air and flew up overhead.

"Like that." Gage pointed up to where Clax hovered barely visible.

"Oh." Wynd looked up and rolled her eyes at Clax. "Why didn't you think of it before? Would have saved us some work."

"Well, we thought of it now. And it's going to make things a whole lot easier."

"Go on then. Let's see what you can do." Wynd waved her hand at Clax.

Clax flashed red and jangled an ugly sound.

"And don't let Cutter catch you. Who knows what he'd do. Likely put you in a cage on display and charge people to gawk—"

Clax flew up and out of sight before she could finish.

"Don't know why you have to go and antigony Clax like that."

"Antagonize." Wynd huffed. "It's antagonize. And *it* started it."

Chapter Twenty-Two
Bad Company

The day dragged on. But, with Clax taking the lead, tracking Cutter became a lot easier. And they could stay farther back. They slipped along the streets, snaking down alleys and creeping between buildings. Clax zipped back to find them and let them know each time Cutter turned down a different lane.

Night closed in and the streets Cutter traveled grew narrower and dingier. But the dirty rotter just strolled along, as if he had no place to be other than walking along a dimly lit lane after dark. He kept his eyes forward, though, like a man who knew exactly where he was going. When he reached the end of Canner's street, he glanced over his shoulder. Gage and Wynd, who had let themselves get a bit too close, ducked behind a stack of old crates and held their breath.

"Ding-dangit," Gage hissed.

Wynd leaned toward the edge of their tuck-up

and peered out.

"Is he still there?"

She ducked back behind the crates and shook her head. "Can't see him. Canner's deadends right where he stopped, though. So, he had to go left or right."

"I know that, but we can't just go strolling 'round the corner to see which way he turned." Gage rubbed the side of his face. "Clax," Gage whispered, "you think you can scout up some more and catch a look at which way the constable went?"

Clax jingled a yes and zipped up into the air.

"Don't let him hear you." Wynd added.

Clax jangled out something ugly before whirring off into the darkness.

Gage rolled his eyes.

"What?" Wynd asked.

He shook his head. "And you don't know why Clax hates you so."

"Because it hates to be wrong?" Wynd slouched against the side of a crate.

"I think that's you." Gage smirked.

"Is not," Wynd said. "Besides, I rarely am." She said the last bit under her breath. But her thoughts turned to her brother Micah and all the times they'd argued. All the times they'd gotten so angry they hadn't spoken for days at a time. What she wouldn't give to have Micah and Jasp back. She'd never yell at them again. At least, she'd try not to.

"You all good?" Gage asked, startling her out of her thoughts.

"Of course." She worked her filter mask up over her mouth and nose.

Gage shook his head. "'Course." The constant layer of smoke and haze had dropped low, clinging to the ground, but he refused to copy Wynd's actions. No sense giving her another reason to think she knew everything.

They waited in silence, the chill damp seeping in though their thin clothes. Finally, they heard a high buzzing, like the sound of skeeters, overhead, and Clax dropped down in a shiny blur of wings and landed on the ground between them.

"Did'ja see 'im?" Gage asked.

Clax flashed blue.

"Well, which way did he go?" Wynd asked.

Clax looked down its nose at Wynd, no mean feat for such a tiny creature. Then stretched out an arm and pointed toward the docks.

A shiver that had nothing to do with the cold snaked its way up Wynd's spine. "It just had to be the docks."

"Dockers turf," Gage muttered. "Clogged stacks and clattering valves! Now, we got Cutter *and* the Dockers to deal with all at once."

Wynd squared her shoulders. "Nothing for it." Micah and Jasp were counting on her.

Gage reached down and held out a shaking hand to Clax, allowing it to climb up and tuck itself inside his jacket cuff.

"At least, there ought to be some places to duck into along the way to keep from being spotted." Wynd pulled her frayed coat tight around her.

"Oh, yes," Gage grumbled. "There are also many great places to jump out from and grab a holt of a couple of lone fools wandering off their own turf."

Wynd frowned. "We can't quit, now. Like you said, Cutter's the best lead we've got. And now he's practically telling us the pits and water bits are connected."

Gage let out an annoyed huff, his face a mask of determination. "Wasn't suggesting we quit. Just saying we're heading into Dockers' home ground. And we had best be on our guard if we want to keep our skins intact." Reluctantly, he wrapped his ragged filter cloth over his face. He wished for his breather for about the zillionth time and glanced over at Wynd, wondering why she didn't have hers with her, either. Lostuns' rule number one: Never get caught out without a breather. No telling when the heavy smog might clout up the air and make it impossible to catch a lungful. He shrugged. Maybe the Dartlings had a different order of rules.

Wynd nodded. "Let's go."

They slunk along the lonely street, as silent as shadows. Even Clax kept dark and quiet, tucked up inside Gage's sleeve.

They paused at the end of the narrow way where it met up with a wide lane. A few crickety wagons full of goods trundled to and from the warehouses. Ahead lay the docks and wharves and beyond them the dark harbor dotted with the lights of ships at anchor.

Out on the nearest rickety dock, they spied Cutter hunched against the cold wind coming off the dark water. They pasted themselves up against the rough wall of a weathered building and stared across the way, as two men approached the copper. One was tall and lanky. He stood erect and walked with the click-clack of well-made shoes, a fancy feathered hat perched atop his head. The other, a sturdy, muscular man who curved over into a low hunch as if expecting an attack at any moment, dipped and swayed like a sailor who never got his land legs.

Gage nudged Wynd. "I think I recognize one of them."

"From where?" Wynd squinted into the darkness. "Thought you stayed away from Dockers turf," she accused.

"I do. Mostly."

Wynd pushed herself harder against the rough

wall of the warehouse. "But desperate times...?"

Gage nodded. "Dispirited measures."

"Close enough," Wynd said. "What were they doing out here the last time you seen 'em?"

"It weren't here." Gage paused recalling that night. Should he tell her about Hannigan? About the weapon?

"Where then? And did you hear anything about our mates?"

"Didn't manage to catch much. I was busy not getting seen." Gage shivered, recalling the exploding water barrel. "Asides, that was before they up and started disappearing."

"Well, I'm as sure as soot, Cutter knows something." Wynd set her jaw.

"And we need to know what he knows," Gage agreed. "Just not sure how we can get close enough to hear what they're sayin'."

"I've an idea," Wynd said. "But I don't think you're going to like it." Her voice dropped to where it was almost impossible to hear. "I know, I don't."

Chapter Twenty-Three
Something Fishy

They crept along the water's edge, to where Clax had settled on a rock, glowing just the faintest blue to show them the way.

They'd had to move quickly to skirt behind the large warehouse and put enough distance between them and the men to make it across the wide edge of the dock without being seen.

"They still there?" Gage said, squinting into the dark. Clax's faint light brightened just a titch. "Right, then. I suppose we're doing this."

Wynd sighed. "Not going to lie. I don't care to go back into that water again." She tried not to breathe too deeply of the dockside stench of old garbage, human and animal waste, and rotted fish guts.

"Don't blame you. Aside from the cold, it's nasty. No wonder Dockers stink so."

"Don't know how they can stand to huddle," Wynd said as she watched Gage turn and pick his way along the rough rocks down toward the water.

Gage glanced up at her and shivered. "Got to keep warm to survive, eh? That's why we have our gangs. That, and they's family."

"Right." Wynd bit her lip. She still hadn't fessed up about leaving her gang in order to find her brothers. She'd tried to enlist the help of her mates to search for her brothers, but without Micah and Jasp, she'd been two votes down, and the tally had not gone her way. They'd made her choose. Them or Micah and Jasp. The Dartlings, well, they'd been a safer choice than loning it, and they had been *like* a family, but— Micah and Jasp were her *real* brothers. The choice was made in her veins.

"Pssst." Gage was halfway to the dark, oily water.

Wynd backed over the edge to follow. The jagged rocks pressed into her cold hands as she clung to them. Reaching down, one foothold, one handhold at a time, she inched her way down until her foot slipped on something slimy. She hung from her fingertips as she frantically sought purchase for her feet again. Something jarred loose and slithered and slapped its way down the rocks. It slid into the water with a gurgling splash before she managed to regain her footholds.

"Careful," Gage warned. "They'll hear us."

She pressed herself close to the rock wall, heart pounding like the chug-chugging of a stampeding steam cart. She shut her eyes and let the cold damp of the rocks seep into her and slow her racing heart, waiting for the beam of a lantern to pierce the shadows and expose them.

Below her, Gage stilled.

Raised voices carried across the water. They sounded hollow, like voices carried through the speaking tubes in the big factories. But when she closed her eyes and listened, she could just make out the words they were saying.

116

"I told you to bring me another brace of street hares. You're one hare shy. Where's the last of them?"

"But I brung ya all them others," the other voice replied. It sounded like Cutter, but Wynd couldn't be certain.

"I am not interested in the others. I am interested in what you still owe me."

"I had 'im in my sights, I did. But the little weasel got away."

"I amn't paying you for excuses. Shields, tell the man. Do I pay for excuses?"

There was the sound of someone chortling. "Nay, Cap'n. Nay."

Wynd's foot slid down and collided with Gage's hand, mashing it against the sharp rock edges. He hissed in pain. "Stay still," he ordered.

She stopped moving and hung above him in silence, but the distraction had caused her to miss some of what the men had said. She'd caught the word "island" and what sounded like "cayno," but she couldn't connect the meanings of the two words.

"...dig my plunder," the first voice said. "Small hands, like we agreed. Do I need to have Shields freshen your memory as to what happens when I don't get value for payment."

"Aye, sir. I mean, no sir." The groveling voice that replied was definitely Cutter's.

"Good then. I'll expect another brace before we set sail on the morning tide."

"But I was only a single short."

"That may as be, but the stock you've been bringing has been subpar. Practically skeletal, that last one. So, in order to make amends, you'll bring me another brace."

Wynd gripped tighter to the rocks and turned her head to see the men over her shoulder.

They stood on the dock in the flickering lantern

light. Three silhouettes, faces shadowed. Cutter's fleshy bulk, the awkward figure of the hunched man, and a tall slender shape.

"But it's late. They'll be hard ta find before they're hunkered in for the night," Cutter complained.

"Shields, tell this cretin that I do not accept failure."

"The Cap'n does not accept failure." The hunched man cleaned his nails with a glinting knife.

Cutter opened his mouth to speak.

The tall man raised a long finger and gazed skyward, as if waiting for something.

The Captain's man looked up from his task and waved his blade in Cutter's direction. "Cap'n Spindle does not enjoy repeating himself."

Cutter stiffened.

The Captain cupped a hand behind an ear. "Now, what was it you were saying?"

Cutter eyed the knife and bowed his head. "Aye, sir. Very well, sir." He ground out the words between his teeth.

"That's what I thought. Then be about it."

"Be about it." The hunched man waved his knife in dismissal.

Gage and Wynd hung from the cold rocks as one of the figures scurried off.

"Think he'll fill out the order?" the round-backed man asked.

"Oh, I think he'll do well to not disappoint me," the tall one responded before click-clacking his way across the dock.

Chapter Twenty-Four
Worth a Gamble

"Well, at leastways we know what's happened to our mates." Gage hissed as Wynd wrapped a strip of fabric around his bloody fingers while Clax buzzed overhead waving its arms. "And we didn't have to get wet, after all."

"You think they were talking about them?" Wynd asked. Then she turned to Clax. "Stop fussing at me. I know what I'm doing."

Clax flared red, waggled its head and chimed something at Wynd in a mocking tone. Then the clockwork flew down to settle on Gage's knee, took a wide legged stance, tiny hands on its hips, and glared up at Wynd.

"Who else d'you think he'd call 'street hares'? And Cutter's been dogged and driven on catching one of us since I woke yesterday. Ouch!" Gage jerked his hand away.

"Hold still," she ordered, reaching for his hand. "Anyway, what's new about that? He's always trying to toss one of us into the workhouse."

"True enough." Gage extended his hand and gritted his teeth. "But I know my gang. If they was in the workhouse, they'd of 'scaped back out or leastwise gotten word to us." He shook his head. "Not to mention, my guts would know if they were as near as the workhouse. And then there's Nobs. Not like him to leave the old 'taker at St. Petra's to do all the work. Though I never have got him to tell why. 'Sides, doncha think the workhouse is the first place I checked?"

"Right," Wynd agreed. She had done the same, a few weeks back, sneaking up close several nights running, and whispering to the littles that stayed for their bit of gruel and hard labor, rather than live on the streets. No one had seen either of her brothers, nor heard a whisper about them. "We know what's happening to them, but not why." She tied off the makeshift bandage and Clax whirred into the air to inspect her handiwork.

"Why do you think?" Gage asked, his face gone all serious. "Small hands for digging out plunder. Though, can't quite figger as why they'd need small hands. Seems like digging plunder'd be more of a big job."

"I suppose it depends on the plunder." Wynd sat back and blinked at him. "So, they're...slavers?" The word choked out of her.

"Dunno." Gage examined his bandaged arm in thought. "Doubt they're paying a working wage, though. And, since no one seems willing to offer us any information, and old Cutter is twistier than coiled braids, there's only one sure way to find out."

"What's that?"

"Stowing away on the smuggler's next run."

Wynd sputtered, but managed to keep her voice low. "You really think getting ourselves smuggled to wherever they're headed on a leaky old boat is the best plan?"

"Do you have a better plan? Asides, you told me the Whisperer said they was across some water. So, that's where we've got to get, someway. You think the better option would be to turn ourselves into a brace for Cutter?"

Wynd dragged her teeth over her bottom lip. The idea of setting foot on a boat curled her insides, but if Micah and Jasp were being slaved somewhere out there, she couldn't turn aside. "But stowaway on a smugglers' ship? Not my first choice." Nor my last, she thought.

"Maybe we could grow wings like Clax and just fly there. 'Course we'd have to know where we were going then, wouldn't we?" Gage cradled his bandaged hand to his chest.

Clax wagged a finger at Wynd and tinkled, mimicking the sound of Gage's voice.

"Fine." Wynd pursed her lips together and blew her breath in the little fairy's face, causing Clax to leap back and streak upward in a flurry of wings and flying sparks. Wynd smiled. "Oh, nice."

"Stop that," Gage grumbled.

"It's not hurting it."

"Don't know why you can't just get a long," he muttered.

"Maybe you should tell it to keep out of my face," Wynd snapped back in annoyance. "Don't know why it hates it so, anyway. Not like it breathes air. Does it? Not to mention, the sparks look pretty."

"Even so, it could draw attention." He pointed out across the docks to where the local smugglers huddled together gambling. Lamplight flickered around them and smoke curled from someone's pipe.

"They'll just think it's sparks from a steamer engine." Wynd countered, as she watched the men throw dice against one of the large boxes that waited loading.

"Which there hain't none of nearby." Gage pointed out.

Wynd frowned. "So?"

"Might be one of 'em knows so and that could send 'em to look into who might be lurking hereabouts. Any rate, we need to get closer. See if we can figger out which ship belongs to that Captain Spindle fellow." Gage beckoned her to follow.

***

They crept along the dock, keeping to the shadows. They'd just reached the edge of the warehouse when a clatter of footsteps clomped along the wooden boards of the dock. Wynd clamped her mouth shut and slid backward into the deeper shadows that hugged the outer wall of the decrepit building. She wriggled her nose against the stink of dead fish that clung to everything like the damp fog clung to the city.

The footsteps closed in, then turned and headed away again and she let out the breath she'd been holding. She leaned away from the rancid stink of the wooden building and wondered what it might be like to smell green plants and trees again rather than the the choking smoke of Landings. She longed to see the sun shining every day, to feel its warmth bathe her face without the wetness that clung to everything in the lower parts of the city.

Gage nudged her and she almost yelped in surprise, her breath hissing out like a tea kettle before he clapped a hand over her mouth.

"What's at?" One of the men raised his shaggy red head and glanced around.

"Don't even try it," snarled another. "Not falling

for it, this time, am I?"

"Not trying anything, just heard a noise is all." The red-headed smuggler continued to scan the dock.

"Sure, ya did. Just like the last time you was losin'."

The sound of dice being thrown hard against the dock rattled out across the water. "Hey, now. That roll don't count."

"The hang it don't." The other man reached for the money that lay on the planks.

The shaggy-headed man raised his foot and stomped down on the money and several fingers.

"Ow! Watch it, there." The kneeling man yelped and yanked his hand out from under the other man's boot.

The third smuggler let out a harsh laugh. "New meaning to tossing the finger-bones." His beady eyes gleamed in the lamplight.

"Shaddup!" The kneeling man barked, shaking his hand as if it had been burned.

"Toss didn't count," said the shaggy one. "Do 'er again."

"Did so. Bandy there saw it. Toss was fair and you both knows it. Now, get your clodhopping boot off my money."

Wynd bit her lip when Gage shook his head at her and pointed. Sliding one foot in front of the other, she did as he bid, slipping as quickly and quietly as possible behind a stack of rotting barrels that stank even more of fish than the rest of the place while the angry men continued to bicker.

"Bandy din't see nothing, did ya Bandy?" The shaggy smuggler said, his voice taking on a dangerous note. But he kept his foot on the coins.

"Did so! Tell him."

Something glinted in the shadows, a flicker of

metal that flashed and disappeared as the shaggy man whipped his arm out and back.

"Oy! You cut me!" The man who had been kneeling was suddenly on his feet. One hand was clasped to his cheek, the other grasping for something in his waistband.

"Don't do it, Sails," Bandy warned, stepping back out of harm's way. "You know Red don't never lose with that blade."

"There's a first time for ever'thing," Sails growled, his own knife now freed of its sheath and glinting in the pale light of the oil lamp hanging from the tall dock post.

Bandy backed farther away, his heels nearly in the shadows where Gage and Wynd now hid. He was so close, Wynd could smell his foul ripeness over the fish stench. She forced herself to breathe in and out as quietly as a mouse, hoping his attention wouldn't stray from the fight taking place on the dock.

Red refused to move his foot from the coins, which made for a rather awkward fight, but he still proved to be the better of the two men with a blade. He ducked and thrust and sliced at his opponent each time Sails got within striking distance.

Sails jumped in and out of the other man's reach so fast he didn't have a chance to get close to cutting Red before he leaped back out of slicing range.

"Good one, Red. Oh, you almost had him that time, Sails. Good duckin'," Bandy cheered them both on from the sideline.

"Leave off." Red tried to slide the money along the dock with his foot, but the coins caught on the rough wood and refused to budge.

"You leave off." Sails leaped in close and away again, his breath huffing in and out.

Red grinned. "I could do this all night, ya know."

"You tell 'im, Red." Bandy hooted and slapped his

knee.

"I can do this till the tide comes in again," Sails huffed back.

"That's right, Sails. Tell it."

Red leaned forward. "You're a liar."

"Ooooh. What says ya to that, Sails?"

"Shut up!" Both of them turned on the beady-eyed smuggler.

"I say we gut him and split the money," Red said, pointing a thumb at Bandy.

Sails nodded, then leaned over to catch his breath.

Bandy jumped back. "Oy, I wasn't in this fight."

"Naw. But ya sure seem keen on seeing blood." Red waved his knife in Bandy's direction.

The tall man in the plume-covered hat stepped around the corner of the building, high-heeled boots click-clicking on the wooden dock. "Do your gutting and spitting on your own time." He pinched a bit of snuff out of a small silver box that glittered with gems and tapped it with the fingers of his right hand. His thin fingers gleamed with rings and jewels as he raised the snuff to his left nostril and sniffed noisily.

The three sailors stopped and turned to face the newcomer, faces filled with sneering anger.

"Who'er you?" Red asked, his knife still at the ready.

The tall man stopped in his tracks, a slender hand going to his chest. "Who am I? Who am I? Shields?"

"Cap'n Spindle here is your new cap'n," the hunched man said as he stepped out from behind the tall man.

"Says who?" Sails demanded.

"Says me." The burly man whipped out his blade and lunged forward, whipped the point through the air, and leaped back quicker than a frog's tongue could snap hold of a juicy fly.

"Owww!" Sails yelled as his belt flapped to the

dock and his pants slipped downward. His knife fell with a clank. He clutched his belly with one hand and gripped at his pants with the other.

"Shields? It seems your aim was off."

"It's nought, but a scratch." Shields grinned wickedly, one silver tooth glinting. "He's not as thin as I took him for."

"Ah, well then." The tall man stroked his long mustache. "I s'pose it couldn't be helped."

"Couldn't be helped?" Still holding his trousers up in one fist, Sails held up his other hand. "I'm bleeding."

The other two smugglers stood watching, mouths hanging open.

In the nearby shadows, much too close for Wynd's liking, she and Gage kept their own mouths shut, not daring to make a sound.

"You'll live. Most likely."

"Most likely? He's our shipmate." Red stepped forward, taking his foot off the coins they'd been fighting over. "Bilge-sucking shark that he is."

Bandy made as if to grab the money, but a snarl from Red stopped him dead.

Shields swung his sword toward Red and Bandy, making a zig-zaggy motion in the air with the tip of the blade.

The sailors watched the glittering blade as if it were a serpent preparing to strike. "'At's right, boys. Keep yer eye on her. She's as fickle as a woman." He laughed, each chuckle wheezing out of him like a sputtering teakettle.

"Calm yourself, Shields. You know what happens when you get excited."

The burly man breathed as if his lungs were full of steam. "Aye, I knows, Cap'n. I knows." He pounded a fist against his wheezing chest, the tip of his blade still hovering before the smugglers. "You boys don't twitch."

"What about me?" Sails whined. "I needs a surgeon." His hand was back on his middle where blood still dripped, soaking into and discoloring his shirt.

"Scourie'll have to knit you up. We're shipping off at first light." Shields waved his sword in the direction of a dark ship moored out on the Deep Ends dock.

"Where to?" Bandy asked.

"Our very own secret island—"

"Our heading is none of your business," the Captain cut Shields off. "Just you do your part and you'll get paid good and proper."

Captain Spindle reached up and placed a forefinger against the side of his nose. "Tasks undone and time's no brother to any man."

"Huh?" Red squinted at him.

Shields huffed, one eye twitching. "What the Cap'n means is, there's work to do and time's a wastin'."

The three men stared.

"Haul up and fall to work, ya blinking barnacles!" Shields shouted.

The three men hustled across the dock and disappeared into the shadows, money and dice forgotten on the planking now stained with drops of red.

Shields leaned down and grabbed up the coins, then kicked the dice to send them skittering across the dock and into the water.

A moment of silence hung in the air. Then something huge and gleaming rose up out of the water with a grinding roar.

Captain Spindle stumbled back, arms raised up over his head. His boots clacked and clattered against the planking as he scrambled up against the warehouse.

The monster fell back into the sea. A wave of

water splashed onto the dock and gushed over the Captain's boots. "Stop it, Shields! Keep it away." The Captain shook so hard his ring-covered fingers rattled against the warehouse wall.

"It's alright, Cap'n. It smelt blood is all. Not to worry. It's all washed away now."

In the nearby shadows, Gage and Wynd crouched in horror.

"What was'at?" Gage mumbled.

A tiny tinging sound came from where Clax shivered inside his pocket.

"I don't know," Wynd whispered. "But we better get up off this dock before it comes back."

Chapter Twenty-Five
Stowed Away

"You want me to climb inside where?" Wynd stepped back.

"It's only for a short spot." Gage worked to pry the lid from the box as silently as he could. Clax hovered close, giving off just enough light to help him see.

Wynd shook her head, a stubborn look on her face. "Not getting inside...that...especially not with you and that little stabber." She pointed at Clax.

"Sshhhh, someone will hear you."

Clax glowed a bright red.

"And you stop that, too," Gage scolded the fairy. "Someone'll see and head straight over to press us to a labor gang."

"At least then we won't have to ride inside a box." Wynd sniffed. "Bad enough being on a boat."

"It's a ship."

"What?"

"A boat is...smaller."

"It goes away from land and out to sea. Who cares

what it's called?"

"Tell an old salt their ship is a boat and they're like to care enough to keelhaul you."

The lid finally came free and Gage started to empty out the contents. "Here." He handed a sack of something to Wynd. "Pour this out over the side of the dock. But do it slow so's not to make a splash."

Wynd took the sack from him and stabbed a hole in it with her sharpened stick, letting the contents spill out into the water. "Shame to waste good cornmeal," she muttered.

"Well, there's plenty more stuff in here, including some dried meat, looks like." He grinned at her across the crate. "Leastways, we won't starve on the way."

"Starving's not the problem."

"What is then?"

She stared out across the dark water. "Never mind. It's fine."

"You sure? 'Cause if it hain't that important to you—"

"I said, it's fine."

Gage shrugged as if he didn't care, but an odd sense of relief settled over him.

Once they'd dumped out enough of the food, Wynd and Gage pushed aside the remaining stores and scrunched down inside the wooden box. Then they pulled the lid back into place, using the ropes Gage had attached to the inside.

"Lid's on good and tight," Gage whispered.

"Darker than midnight," Wynd murmured, her voice rough.

"Close fit." Gage adjusted his arms and legs and shifted away from Wynd.

"I don't know. I think it's kinda cozy." Wynd elbowed him in the ribs, then snickered.

"Very funny," Gage mumbled, wishing he'd made

that joke.

Clax's wings buzzed and a faint red glow lit up the small space.

"Oh, just like candle light. Very romancey," Wynd said.

Clax jangled, its glow deepening to a dark maroon.

Something stomp-dragged its way across the wooden planks of the dock.

"Shhhhhh," Gage warned. "Someone's coming."

The sounds drew closer. Then something heavy thumped down on top of their crate.

They sat as still as the statues in Landings's central gardens. Gage felt Wynd shiver beside him, but he didn't dare move. Something tapped against the box. A moment later, they heard a soft whooshing sound, and the scent of burning tobacco drifted in between the wooden slats.

Gage covered his face. The smell of bitter smoke reminded him of the old director at the orphans' workhouse the one time he'd been caught and Cutter had dragged him kicking into the place. Just recalling the lashings he'd taken before he'd had a chance to escape made Gage's bum smart. He started to shift his weight just as someone snorted loudly and spat something nasty into the sea.

"Hoy!" A gruff voice shouted. "Get up and heave to. No one's payin' ya ta smoke and spit, ya rusty cog."

Above them, the wooden lid creaked. There was a loud sound of someone letting go a bellyful of gas. The man sitting on the crate sighed in contentment.

Wynd gripped Gage's arm and he barely contained the snort of laughter that burbled up inside him.

"Hang on ta yer bloomers," the man outside the box hollered. He let out another ripper, then heaved himself off the box.

"Oy! What'choo bin eatin'?" someone asked.

The other sailor cackled in glee. "Just go on t'other side and help me heave 'er aboard."

The box tilted and rose into the air. Wynd and Gage braced themselves against the wooden sides to keep from tumbling into one another.

"This one is heavy," one of the men complained.

"You've got no muscles, Noodles. Ever'body knows that."

"I'll show you no muscles."

The box rocked from side to side.

"Stop fooling' about. You'll dump the whole mess."

"Who cares? Prolly just maggoty hardtack."

"I cares. You didn't see what the new Cap'n's man did to Sails, just for speaking out. Dump the load and we'll get what for. I hain't taken no punishment on account of you can't haul your own weight."

"Say that again once we've stowed this on board and we'll see who hasn't got no muscles."

"Shut it, you two, and finish up," someone growled. "I got a date with a tankard over at the Muddy Crawler."

"Fine, fine."

The box swayed and leaned as the men hauled it up the gangplank, their bare feet slapping against the decking. Wynd gabbed Gage's arm, as the box swung up and then landed with a thud. Ropes slithered against the outside. Then, the box creaked and a steam hauler hissed as they were lifted into the air where they dangled, swinging back and forth.

Clax hid its face inside Gage's sleeve. The red glow of its fear and displeasure blushed against his wrist. Beside him, Wynd sat stiff and hunched, barely breathing.

The rope jerked and the box shuddered, then dropped. Wynd sucked in her breath as the box lurched to a stop and swung like a pendulum. Someone cursed. Wynd clamped her jaw shut, crossing her fingers against bad luck, hoping they wouldn't get dropped.

Finally, the box stopped swinging and they began moving again.

After being lowered into the damp darkness, the box clunked onto the wooden planking of what must be the ship's hold. Gage pricked up his ears as the ropes were undone and slithered off the crate. More footsteps and the lifting and heaving of the box told him they had been successfully loaded onto the ship and stowed. The footsteps receded, but just as he opened his mouth to congratulate himself aloud, there was more jostling and thudding outside the box. They waited in silence as the sailors finished loading the ship.

"'At's the lot, is it?" one of the men asked.

"Aye, and I for one am glad. There's still some drinking hours left," another said as they climbed up out of the hold with a clatter of feet on the ship's wooden ladder.

"They've gone," Gage whispered after a long silence. "And we're safe on board."

Wynd shifted to kneeling. "On board, yes. But I wouldn't call this safe." Her voice shook. "We need to find a better place to hide before they come back." She sat up and pushed at the lid. "That's not funny, Gage," she growled. "Let go of the ropes."

"I ain't holdin' 'em." He pushed at the lid, but it didn't budge. "Curse it all, I think something heavy got loaded on top."

Chapter Twenty-Six
Boxed In

"Oh, that's just fine," Wynd huffed. When they'd been in control of holding the lid down, the box hadn't seemed so tight. Now, with no way out, the sides of the thing seemed to close in on her. "We're stuck in this box for who knows how long." Her breathing grew rapid. "What if we hit a storm? What if—"

"Shhhhh," Gage hissed. "Someone'll hear you, and this box won't be nothing compared to the one we end up in."

"Not helping," Wynd grumbled, but she squished her eyes shut and forced her breathing to slow. "So, what do we do now?"

"I'm thinking."

"Well, think faster."

Clax crawled out of Gage's sleeve and settled on his hand. The fairy gave off a faint bluish glow that cast a pale light inside the small dark space and buzzed its tiny wings.

"What?" Gage asked.

"I didn't say anything," Wynd said.

"Not you. Clax. It's trying to tell me something, but I can barely make out its chimes most the time and now with just this wing buzzing bizzyness..."

Wynd opened one eye and stared. The fairy stood in the faint blue aura, wings buzzing. Finally, Clax unsheathed its sword and gestured at the side of the box.

Wynd put a hand behind her ear, then shook her head. "I think it's...whispering. But I don't understand."

The clockwork tossed its hands up in frustration, then pointed at Gage and back at itself before making a series of gestures.

Gage watched Clax's movements. "Oh!" he said, finally.

"Oh, what?" Wynd asked.

"You want me to whittle a hole on the side of the box, so you can go see what's keeping the lid on. Is 'at right?"

"Huh?" Wynd shook her head.

Clax nodded, head bobbing in the pale blue light.

Gage pulled out his small, nicked pocketknife. He slid his fingertips along the sides of the box, then stopped. "Clax, put some of that light over here, will ya?"

Clax glowed, luminating the outline of a knothole, and Gage dug into the ready-made grooves with the short blade. Little by little, he whittled away small slices of wood until the hole finally widened enough for Clax to fit through. It perched on the edge of the hole and peered out, then, in a blink and a flutter, was gone. Gage and Wynd waited in the darkness, while time moved like sold gear oil, slow and sluggish.

Finally, the clockwork fairy returned, scooting back through the small opening. Clax's wings buzzed in the same whispery way as before, but this time the sound was accompanied by more mime acting.

"Clax says most of the sailors have gone... dockside, I think, to spend their last night ashore, drinking and gambling and...um..." Gage glanced at Wynd, then looked away. "I'm not repeating that last bit."

Clax flashed blue with a jingling titter, then buzzed its wings some more.

"Anyway, the few left aboard are on watch or asleep."

"Wonderful. I'm so happy for them," Wynd said. "How's that help us get out of this box?"

Clax buzzed again.

"There's a heap of sacks piled on top of us. If we do manage to raise the lid, we'll have to do it careful, or the noise will raise the watch."

Wynd sighed. "Any suggestions?"

"I suppose we could remove some of the side slats and get out that way." Gage mused.

"Maybe. But how do we put them back into place after? A crate that's been opened from the inside is going to make for a lot of questions and likely a ship-wide search."

"Oh. I hadn't thought of that." Gage slouched against the side of the crate. "If we only knew how long the trip was, we'd at least know if we need to get out of the crate sooner or later."

"I've heard," Wynd said, her mouth dryer than it should be, "that there are some voyages that take half a year or more."

"I doubt we're headed that far," Gage said. "Seems they'd not be back so soon after taking our mates, eh?"

"About that," Wynd said, her throat tight. "Promise you'll help my...my mates get away from the smugglers, no matter what happens."

"What?"

"I...I want to extend our pact beyond working together. I want it to include helping one another's mates...no matter what happens. I mean..."

"I know what you mean," Gage said, his voice low and serious. "I'll swear, if you will."

"I swear," Wynd said. "Hand to heart. No spit needed."

"Done."

"Thanks."

They grew quiet.

"How long do you think we'll be stuck in here before they need their food supplies?" Wynd finally asked.

"Don't know. They might have all they need in the galley or elsewhere. What was in this box may have been set aside for when they make landfall."

Wynd tried not to think about how long it might take for a ship to reach another shore. Her father's ship had been out to sea for over a month before...

"Seems as like they said we were headed for some island. And I've heard tell as there are heaps of islands stretched across the ocean."

Wynd sagged against the side of the crate and tried not to think about it. But the harder she tried, the more her head filled with the vast, ominous sea.

Chapter Twenty-Seven
Anchors Aweigh

They sat in silence for a long stretch. The ship floating beneath them rocked with the waves, lulling them toward sleep.

With a start, Wynd jerked awake. "Wait. Clax said there were sacks on top of the crate?"

"So?"

"Any idea what's in them?"

"What's it matter?" Gage grumped.

"I was just thinking that if Clax could cut a hole in one or two of the sacks—"

Gage picked up her thought. "Then maybe some of what's inside could sift out—"

"And lighten up the weight—"

"So's we can push up the lid," Gage finished.

Before they'd done talking over one another, Clax had squeezed out through the hole in the side of the crate and flown off. Soon, there came the sound of something sifting down the side of the box. First, one trickle and then another, and another...

Clax reappeared at the opening, glowing a bright blue and jingling merrily.

"Shhhh. Tone it down," Wynd said.

With an angry buzz, the clockwork's glow winked out.

"Hey," Gage said. "Clax was just excited."

"Sorry. But it won't be so excited if we get caught."

"You think they'll make us swab the decks and work for our passage?" Gage scoffed.

"You think they won't have any worse ideas of things to do with a couple of stowaway throwaways?"

"Hain't a throwaway," Gage groused. "I just..."

"Just what?" Wynd asked.

"Nuffin'."

"We're all throwaways to people like Cutter. And these smugglers."

Gage pushed up on the lid and felt it give just a bit. "It's working. Thank you, Clax." He nudged Wynd with his elbow.

"Thank you, Clax." Wynd rubbed her ribs where he'd elbowed her. "And thank you, Wynd, for the excellent idea." She elbowed him back. "Do you think we maybe should wait?"

"Wait? For what?" Gage pushed at the lid once more and it lifted even higher.

"Well, we haven't even set sail, yet. We don't want them to find us while we're still in port and just kick us off the ship before we find out where they're taking my...our mates."

Gage let the lid down with a quiet thump. "Not like they'll welcome us aboard if they find us whilst we're out at sea. Fact is, they'll likely make us walk the plank."

"That's pirates, not smugglers," Wynd said, trying not to sound frightened.

"Not much difference a'tween 'em, I'd say. But you may be right. Might be best not to be stumbling about afore we heave off."

Wynd pictured herself standing high above the raging sea at the end of a wooden plank while the man with the long thin sword swiped his blade through the air to force her closer and closer to the end. "Then again, we might want to be scarce if they decide they want dried meat, and come looking and find us instead. There must be better places to hide in than in a box of provisions."

Just then, someone on deck began barking orders. The creaking ship rocked and heaved as the crew weighed anchor. Pistons clacked, the engines whirred to life, and the ship chugged out to sea.

Chapter Twenty-Eight
Caught in the Act

"Now's our chance," Gage said. "Whilst they're all a hubbub gettin' underway. It will give us plenty of time to find a new hidey. Got to be plenty better spots."

Wynd wasn't sure anyplace on the ship would be safe, but she wasn't keen on getting caught in a half-empty box of what should have been food. Though, she stuffed her pockets with as much of the dried beef as she could before agreeing.

Even with the sacks atop their crate emptying out into the hold, it still took both of them to push up the lid.

"Shhhhh." Wynd said as the sacks shifted suddenly, sliding off the lid to land on the deck of the hold with a whump.

They froze, hands still holding the lid of the box open, but there was no sound of approaching feet, nor any indication that the sound had drawn anyone's attention.

After what seemed like forever, Gage spoke. "You go first. I'll hold the lid till you're out."

Wynd nodded, though in the dark hold it wasn't likely he could see her. She pulled herself up and out over the side of the crate, then turned to hold the lid up for Gage when suddenly, there was noise like the jangling of keys behind her, and the heavy tread of large feet climbing down the ladder. It was too late to climb back into the crate. She shoved Gage's hands away from the lid and shut it with a loud bang as she turned to face the smuggler behind her.

"Well now. Wot 'ave we 'ere?" He opened the screen on his lantern and held it out before him. "I come down expecting' to find a skittering' dock rat and instead, I find a cock-a-roachy."

Wynd blinked, squinting into the too bright light of the lantern after the darkness of the box inside the damp hold. "I'm no such thing."

"Oy, my mistake, so merely a loverly little stowaway, then. You know what we do with stowaways, little bug?"

Wynd licked her lips, praying for Gage to stay quiet. If one of them was able to stay hidden, their mates, her brothers, might have a chance. "Something nice, I hope."

"Nice?" The smuggler roared with laughter. "Oh, well, nice for us maybe." He turned to the side and waved his hand with a mocking bow. "After you, little bug. Let's go and see what *nice* thing we can stir up for one such as yerself."

Chapter Twenty-Nine
Aye Spy

Gage sat stunned and still as a rock inside the wooden crate, Clax tucked inside his sleeve. Wynd had shoved him back inside the box and clamped down the lid so fast, he'd had no time to think about why. But now his head spun as he listened to the smuggler laughing and calling Wynd ugly names. She'd saved him. Least, she'd given him a chance. But a chance for what?

And what was going to happen to Wynd? He reached for the lid, but Clax pinched his wrist. He clamped his lips down to keep in the hiss of pain.

They listened to the sound of footsteps moving away. Finally, when he was sure they were alone in the hold, he took a breath. "Ow, Clax. Whyd'ja do that?" He rubbed at his burning wrist. The clockwork climbed up his arm to his shoulder and buzzed all whispery like, but Gage couldn't understand. Finally, it let out an annoyed jingle.

"Right," Gage said, "but we shoulda done

something."

Clax glowed a soft red and shook its head.

"Well, we can't just leave her to those rotters."

Clax shrugged.

"Because, we made a pact, and Lostuns don't break our pacts." But something niggled at him. Why would Wynd give herself up? To keep him from being discovered? Or, might she be planning to give him up instead? Naw, she wouldn't. Would she? Not after everything that had happened. Unless maybe the smugglers could offer her something in trade. Something she really wanted. Like her ding-dang missing mates. Not like he really knew her. Not like she and her gang hadn't broken their word on the turf rumble. She could be up there now telling them all about him. He tried to swallow, but his mouth had gone dry.

The sound of muffled voices drifted down into the hold. He lifted the edge of the lid and strained to hear what was said, but couldn't sift the words. His skin tightened and buzzed with tension. He needed to know what was going on. Needed to know if he was being betrayed. "Clax," he whispered, "think you can go up top and see what's happening?"

Clax flashed blue.

"Be careful," Gage said. Clax was, after all, just a tiny clockwork. "You saw how nasty those smugglers are, cutting their own mates like that on the dock and all."

Clax whipped out its tiny sword, slashed it through the air and raised it in salute. Then zipped out through the hole in the side of the crate.

Chapter Thirty
Trapped Like a Rat

Wynd stood in front of the smugglers' leader, who was also the ship's Captain. He wore a shop's worth of frilly finery. Velvet jacket, silver buttons and buckles, and big shiny rings glittering on every finger. Black locks curled over his shoulders, and the wide brim of a fine plumed hat shaded his narrow face. He sat in a tall-backed wooden chair bolted in place on a high deck at the back of the ship with a clear view of everything. He showed her his teeth in what looked to be part grin, part snarl.

Beside him stood the man called Shields, feet wide, hand on his sword hilt and an ugly gleam in his eyes. Smugglers and sailors surrounded them, though it looked like they were all one and the same.

The steamer ship plowed through the sea like a knife through softened butter. The Captain's fancy dark curls ruffled in the breeze. The sky above was a shade of blue Wynd had never seen in Landings. But the clean air barely registered, because out past the railings and, except for a dark smudge in the distance behind them, all around the ship was frothy water as far as she could see. She'd had no idea a ship could travel so fast, but they plowed across the waves as quicker than a cutpurse escaping the coppers.

She gulped and forced herself not to gape at the wide watery expanse, tried not to let her fear show, but her knees shook and her palms sweated. Bad enough to be surrounded by a dozen dangerous cut-throats, but to be out on the wide ocean with no land in sight, ...Why, they could throw her overboard in a blink and she'd sink like a stone to the bottom of the sea, just like...She shut her eyes against the thought and tried to picture her brothers. She needed to be smart, for their sake.

"Well, well, well." The Captain took out a small box and pinched out some dark powdery snuff, then stuck it to his nose and sniffed. His nose twitched and his eyes watered, but before he could let out a sneeze, Shields whipped out a frilly handkerchief and handed it to him.

The Captain didn't even look Shields, only took the lacy hanky and blew his long nose into it, before flinging it back at the man, who stuffed it into his jacket pocket without a flinch.

"Now, to what do we owe the, ahem, pleasure of your company? What drew you, out of all the possible vessels anchored at Landings docks, to mine. And make it good, or we won't continue to be so pleasant." He snapped his fingers and Shields reached behind the chair and produced a tall bottle and a crystal goblet. He poured a ruby red liquid into the glass and handed it to the Captain, who swirled the liquid and held it up to the light before taking a sip and making a sour face.

Wynd tried to speak, but her thoughts slipped out of her head like eels escaping a fishing net. She couldn't come up with a single story she thought might convince him that her stowing away on this particular ship was a mere coincidence.

"Speak up, before I bore of this." He handed the still full goblet back to Shields, folded his hands together, and twiddled his thumbs as he spoke.

"Tsk, tsk, not a pro-pity-us start." One corner of Shields' mouth turned up in a dangerous half-smile. "Nought worse'n borin' the Cap'n."

"I was only looking to...travel. A ship seemed the, um, easiest way. And what without anyone guarding the gangway..."

"'At's a filthy lie!" one of the men shouted.

"Is it indeed?" The Captain held up one hand, his fine-boned finger pointing to the sky. "Mr. Secons, are you able to confirm that all who should have been on duty were at their posts at all times during the night?"

"Nay, Cap'n." A man to her left answered. "I was on duly assigned shore leave."

"Then who was it had the deck watch?"

"That'd be Mr. Stints."

"Ah. Mr. Stints step forward."

"Stints! Front and central," Shields shouted.

"Aye, Captain?" A thick-armed man with a swaying gait crossed the deck, stopping just inside the circle of men.

"Were all the men at their stations last night?"

Mr. Stints glanced around at the men, his face creased in confusion. "Well, uh..."

"Yes or no? It's a simple question." The Captain had not looked away from Wynd the entire time. "There is a stowaway aboard my ship, and I wish to know if we are a ship of no-good seafaring smugglers, or a lax bunch of landlubbers." His voice took on a menacing tone. "Was my ship guarded as it should have been throughout our stay in port?"

"Uh, yes, Captain." Mr. Stints rubbed his chin with the back of his hand.

"You are a terrible liar." The Captain sighed. "But, to be sure, the men are bound to appreciate the effort. Assign yourself twenty lashes and confinement for the remainder of the voyage."

"But...but..." Mr. Stints sputtered.

"Shall we make it forty?"

"Aye, Captain. I mean, nay, Captain." Stints sagged and lurched away, but not before giving Wynd an evil-eyed glare.

"'Tis a shame the way vermin manage to crawl aboard ships these days. Eh, Shields?"

"Aye, Cap'n," the man at his side said.

"What shall we do with you?" The Captain stroked his curling mustache and stared at Wynd.

Wynd wiped her hands on her ragged pants. "I could work for my passage," she said, trying to sound hopeful.

"Indeed?" The Captain leaned back in his chair. "And what type of shipboard work might you be able to do, pray tell?"

"I can cook."

"Shields, do we have a cook?"

"Aye, Cap'n, 'at we do."

"I...I can sew."

"Do we have men who can sew, Shields?"

"Aye, Cap'n, 'at we do."

"In fact, do we have any openings at all on our crew?" The Captain made a show of examining his fingernails.

Shields frowned, tilted his head back and looked up in thought for a moment. "Nay, Cap'n, ever billet is filled by a able bodied man, excepting Seaman Sails, as he's in the 'firmery with a nasty gash to the stomach."

"Will he recover?"

"Oh, aye, Cap'n. Some miscreants are harder ta kill than most."

"Well then, perhaps we need to do some fumigating."

Shields took a step toward Wynd and she flinched.

Shields smirked and stepped back, and the men all laughed.

Wynd ground her teeth. They were playing with her. She disliked when people discounted her, or treated her like a simpering girl. But she hated it worse when they toyed with her.

She'd seen it before, some fine-dressed fop would come along with his gang of supposed gentleman, and they'd act as if they were about to drop a coin on one of the street urchins. Then they'd whip the coin away and laugh at the disappointment they'd caused. They were the ones the Dartlings waited for. The ones they'd jump from out of an alley and trip to spilling, then pick them clean of every penny before scarpering off.

But here, she had no gang. No one to back her. And these men were armed and dangerous. She stood her ground but bit her tongue.

"Did you have something to say, little vermin?" The Captain leaned forward in his chair, his dark eyes glittering menace beneath the brim of his feathered hat.

"I'd say," Wynd blurted, her tongue moving faster than her wits could control, "that this ship does indeed need to be fumigated."

The Captain sat back startled, and the men around them sucked in their breath.

Wynd bit her tongue, knowing it was too late to take it back.

"A rat that bites with wit." The Captain tilted his head to the side. "Note that in the logbook, Shields."

The Captain leaned back in his chair, crossed his

legs, and pulled out his snuff box, holding it with two fingers and flicking the lid open. But before he dipped another pinch, he raised one slender finger into the air. "Oh, and lock her up with the rest of the vermin. She'll find out all about fumigation when we reach the isle."

Shields snickered. "Aye, Cap'n. That she will."

Chapter Thirty-One
Choosing Sides

Down below, Gage had slipped out of the crate and tucked himself into a dark corner where he peered out, watching from beneath a heap of empty sacks. They smelled like moldery fish guts, but it was the only place he could find that seemed likely to be left unbothered. He for sure wouldn'ta bothered with them if he had any better choice.

When Clax flew back down into the dimly lit hold, Gage let out a hiss to let the clockwork know where he was.

Clax buzzed over and ducked beneath the tent of dirty sacks that Gage had made.

"So?" Gage asked. "What did you see?"

Clax tinkled quietly at him, glowing an odd shade of purple. Then, with a flourish, it acted out two people having a chat, nodding their heads and spitting in their hands for a shake.

"What?

Clax did the spitting handshake again.

"They made a bargain?"

Clax shrugged.

"Are you sure?"

Clax flashed red, but refused to meet his eye.

"Ding-dangity," Gage huffed. "I shoulda knownt it. Good thing I got outta that crate. She's like to be giving me up right now, and they'll be down to yank me out any ding-dang minute. But now what? If they don't find me in the crate, they're bound to search around. And I'm right smack here where they'll likely look first."

Clax put a finger on its tiny chin, and the two of them sat there in thought. A scritch-scratching coming from somewhere behind them made Gage sit up.

Clax put a hand on its sword hilt.

"D'ya think it's rats?" Gage muttered.

Clax shrugged.

Gage pulled out his boot blade and crawled along the edge of the hold, searching for the cause of the sound. He didn't want to be surprised by anything. Especially not a ship's rat. Some of them could be ginormous. "Must be huge to make such a loud noise."

Clax whipped out its tiny sword and struck a defensive pose, then pointed to where the sound was coming from.

"You sure that's a good idea?"

With a flutter of wings, Clax rose into the air, prepared to strike.

"A'right, then." Gage let out his breath and dug behind a stack of ropes. The scratching grew louder as he pushed aside the heavy coils.

Finally, he found the wooden planking beneath the pile.

The scratching continued.

Clax hovered close.

With a scraping noise, something poked up from between two wooden planks. Gage jumped back, knocking into Clax, who did a double aerial somersault. Clax jangled annoyance. But Gage wasn't paying attention to Clax. He was focused on the pointed stick that had popped up between the planks and was sawing up and down, trying to cut through the ship's tarring. There was more hold space beneath them. And someone was down there, poking holes in the decking.

"Pssst," he hissed. "Who's down there?"

The stick stopped moving. Silence, followed by whispers. Then nothing.

"We could maybes help one and another," Gage offered.

A shuffling sound, then a familiar voice spoke. "Gage, is that you?"

Gage gulped. "Wynd?"

Clax grabbed him by the collar and tried to pull him away from the crack in the floorboards.

"Too late for it now, Clax. If we're gave up, then we're already done for." He leaned forward to peer through the narrow space. "What're ya doing down there?"

"Oh, nothing much," Wynd said in a lilting voice. Then her tone changed. "For cogs' sake, they've locked me in. What do you think I'm doing? Having tea and crumpets with the Queen?"

"Well, one might never know what antiques a Dartling'd be up to," he shot back.

"So, that's how it is? After I gave myself up to keep that ugly ruster from catching us both? Fine then. I s'pose you don't want to know I've bumped into some of your mates. Very well. Go on about your business, whatever that might be. And by the way, it's antics, and I'm not up to any."

"Wait. What?" Gage laid himself down on the

153

planking and put an eye to the opening, but the space below was darker then the hold he was in. "Who is it?"

"Ho, Gage," Nobs called out to him and several voices shushed him at once. "Sorry."

"Nobs?" Gage said through the crack.

More shuffling, then Nobs said from right below him, "Yeah, Gage, it's me."

"How'd you end up here?"

"Cutter," Nobs mumbled. "Thought I'd gave 'im the old slip, but when I popped out of the hidey and made for St. Petra's, he was awaitin' for me. It were a stupid mistake. He snagged me up and...and here I am. Sorry he got you, too, Gage."

"He didn't," Gage said. "I...we..."

"What he's trying to say," Wynd spoke up, "is that we came on our own. To try and rescue our mates. And here *we* are." She sighed. "Not much of a rescue."

"Ah, Gage." Nobs sniffed. "Ya shouldn'ta."

In the silence, Gage imagined Nobs nodding and wiping his nose on his sleeve.

"Now, don't go all Checks on me," Gage told him.

"Speaking of..." Nobs said. "You'll never guess who else they got."

"Who?"

"Buttons." Nobs snuffled. "An' Tups—"

"And us, too, Gage," the twin voices of Blimey and Chaser chimed in.

"Right," Nobs said. "Well, pretty much all of us that were left, ay, includin'—"

"Shut it," a familiar voice grumbled.

Surprise washed through Gage. "Checks! They got you too?"

"What of it?" Checks growled.

"Not making anything of it," Gage said. "Just surprised, is all. How'd you end up here?"

"Nabbed grabbing a fat purse, a'course. Was a beauty of a plan, too. Woulda been the take of the century," Checks bragged.

"'Ceptin' for Cutter having a whole barrage of coppers set to pounce on us," Buttons chimed in.

"Well no one coulda rightly planned for that," Checks insisted.

"Right," Wynd said. "Like anyone can believe a word you say."

"Wait up. Don't I know you?" Checks said.

"And I know exactly who *you* are," Wynd shot back.

"Hey," Gage said. "We need to work together, now. Find a way of escape."

They were silent for a long moment.

"Oy, Gage. Shoulda knowed you'd like as show up here," Checks said, finally.

"I couldn't not try to find everyone. We're family, right?"

"Right," Nobs and the others said.

"Anyways, we made a pact. And Lostuns don't break their words. Unlike some others," Gage said.

There was more jostling of bodies, and then Wynd's voice came from right below him. "What's that supposed to mean?"

"It means that I know you're in kaputs with the smugglers."

"I'm what?"

"Don't deny it. I know you've been talking to the Captain and his gang. I expect they'll be coming down here to drag me out any minute."

"You mean, cahoots, and I'm quite certainly, not."

"Clax heard everything. Including your offer to work with them."

"Clax? Did that dingy little trinket also tell you that I was playing for time and maybe a way to get us out of this mess? And that they locked me up in this dank, waterlogged hole in the belly of this nasty, leaky, bound-to-sink, dirty, smuggler-infested, floating coffin? Along with your foul excuse for a gang leader?" Wynd's voice went up in volume as she spoke and a chorus of voices shushed her. "Arrrgh, sorry."

Gage looked over his shoulder to see Clax in the air, arms crossed, eyes glued to the overhead. "Clax?"

With a buzzing of wings, Clax flashed red, then purple, then red again, then shrugged.

Gage shook his head. "You're s'posed to be helping," he scolded.

Clax pointed down to where Wynd was imprisoned, jangled out a sour note, and threw its hands up in the air.

Gage rolled his eyes at the fairy. "Fine, I'm owed as much to blame for not trustin' as you. But we all need to work together from here on out. Hain't that right, Wynd?"

Wynd made a harrumphing noise, and he imagined the annoyed look on her face.

"Checks? What about you?"

"We got plenty of Lostuns here to do what needs done. We don't need no disgustin' Dartlings' help," Checks muttered.

"Hah! Leastways Dartlings aren't liars." Wynd's comment was followed by a loud thump and scuffle.

Gage rubbed the back of his neck at the ruckus below him. "We need to corporate together. Can't you at least wait for a scuffle after we get out of this mess?"

"Fine." Checks spat. "But once we get back to our digs, a scuffle it is."

Silence from the hold told Gage the fighting had stopped, but he could practically feel the burning glares of the two rival gang leaders who faced off below him. "Come on, Wynd. We've came this far together. You goin' ta cut and scarper now? Thought you was prepared to go the distance?"

"Go the distance?" she said. "Then what? Back to the good old days? Back to scuffles and scraps and right out rumbles?"

Gage shrugged, then realized none of those below could see him. "I hain't all in a rush for going back to the way things were, myself. But I sure amn't in a hurry to do hard labor for a gang o' rotten smugglers, are you?"

"Fine," she groused. "I'll *cooperate*. But what do you expect us to do while we're locked in the bottom of this leaking tub?"

"I guess we need to start with a plan," Gage said.

Chapter Thirty-Two
Best Laid Plans

"Tell them what?" Wynd couldn't believe what Gage had just said.

"Tell the Captain you've a message from Cutter. That he wants a bigger cut or he'll turnt 'em all in fer smugglin' and kidnapperin'."

"But he's in on it with them. He's as rotten as they are. Why wouldn't they just threaten to out him for his part in the scheme?"

"Sure, but he's the law, hain't he? Who's goin' ta believe a bunch a thievin' smugglers over a man o' the law, right?"

It made sense in a twisty kind of way. Wynd couldn't argue that, but every time she pictured all that water, she felt like she was already drowning. At least here in the hold, she could try and pretend they weren't out in the middle of the heaving ocean. "They've already threatened to drop me over the side. What's to keep them from tossing me overboard as soon as I open my mouth with such a load of rot?"

"Well, 'at's part of the beauty of the plan," Gage's excited voice dropped down through the crack in the planks. "We need ever'one in the water, any rate. Doesn't really matter how. That's why we wait till they drop anchor and make for going ashore. So's we're not moving and the ship is close up to land."

"Doesn't matter where we are when they throw me into the sea," Wynd grumbled, trying to hide the fear that shook her from her toes all the way to the strands of her tangled hair. "I already told you. I can't swim."

"Me, neither," Nobs mumbled.

"Nor can the rest of us as is locked down here," someone else said.

"I can paddle somes," Tups said.

"Us, too. But we only ever done so near shore," Blimey offered.

"See?" Wynd's stomach unclenched just a bit. "It isn't only me."

"Well, 'at's what me and Clax are for. Clax's already scouted the ins and outs. I'll drop one of the small boats and once ever'one's in the water, we'll pull aside and pick ever'one up. All's you have to do is keep yer noses up."

"This plan is no better than the last seventeen you came up with." Wynd pulled at her hair in frustration.

"Well, none of you have come up with a better," Gage shot back.

Chapter Thirty-Three
Bad Bet

Gage stayed hidden for an unreckonable amount of time, only sneaking across the hold to grab a few sacks of dried meat from the crate they'd stowed away in. "All in all," he whispered down to the others, "could be worser. Leastways, there's food. And meat at that."

He managed to pass some of the ragged strips down through the space they'd widened between the planking, but try as they might, they had no way to pass water up to him from the leaky wooden bucket that had been dropped inside their cell. The best they'd been able to do was to wet a ragged bit of cloth torn from someone's shirtsleeve—Gage hoped it hadn't been Nobs'—and pass the end up to him to suck the wetness from. It wasn't much, but it lessened the pain of his parched tongue as he gnawed at the leathery strips.

The steamer's engine grumbled, props churning against the water. The hold grew colder and darker, and twice a couple of the smugglers clambered down the ladder to shift some of the stores and haul a bag or box up top. Below, in the cell where Wynd and the others were locked, the water bucket had been refilled and a pan of stale biscuits shoved in through the bars, but there was no way to tell how much time passed.

Gage had been dozing herky-jerky like, when Clax pinched his ear to wake him. The clockwork had been keeping a watch out in case any of the crew climbed down into the hold.

"Yowch." He rubbed his ear between two fingers.

Clax buzzed for him to be quiet.

"Pssst. You okay?" Wynd asked from below him.

"Fine," he grumbled, his voice still groggy with sleep.

"What's going on?"

Overhead, voices called out and the slap-slap of feet against the deck signaled movement.

"Not sure," Gage whispered, his mouth right up against the narrow space and his ears cocked at the sound above. "But there's something astir up top."

A short while later, the clomping of heavy footsteps and the grumble of voices rose from below. "Time ta go, my little bric-a-bracs."

"Where to?" Wynd asked, her voice shaky.

"Just you don't never mind yourself about that. You'll see soon enough, I reckon."

"They all still in there?" a voice called from somewhere.

"I dunno."

"Well count, 'em and make sure. I hain't wantin' ta be practice meat for the Cap'n's grinder."

"Fine. How many was there ta start?"

"Six, I think."

"Fine. Oy, you, line up so's we can count ya.

"One, two, three, four, five, six, seven."

"Wait. That's not right. You sure it were six?"

There was a pause before the other voice called back. "Six it were. But then that stubborn one what got Mr. Stints in for lashes. So, that'd be..."

"Seven?"

"Right. Seven."

A rusty metal door groaned open. "March on up the ladder, now. There's a good bunch. Don't plague us with none of yer trouble, and we won't give you none of ours."

"Like we don't have it already," Wynd grumbled just loud enough for Gage to hear. Then she raised her voice. "I'm going. I'm going. No need to shove."

That was Gage's cue. He flung off the ratty burlap sacks he had covered himself with and snuck over to the ladder that led up on deck.

Clax tugged at his collar, but he ignored the anxious buzzing behind his ear.

Above him, the wooden hatch sealed out all but the barest daylight. He climbed up and perched at the top of the ladder and pushed against the hatch. But it wouldn't budge.

Just his luck. He hadn't planned for the hatch to be latched shut. Then again, he hadn't heard it being locked or unlocked when the smugglers had come and gone. Could it just be stuck? He braced himself on the ladder, tucked his knees under him, and prepared to give it a good shove with his shoulder, then heard a voice from right above him.

He froze, and Clax stopped yanking at him, wings quieted.

"Seems like ever' time we get a new bunch of gutterbugs, they're weaker 'an the ones afore."

How long you think this bunch'll last?"

"Dunno," came the reply. "Cap'n has been gettin' less tolerant with 'em. Not ta mention how much he hates ta feed 'em. Says it's less costly just to grab new ones."

"Give you odds this group'll be on their last legs afore the rest."

"Yer on. That last bunch were already raggedy twigs when we brung 'em."

Someone spat followed by the sound of two meaty hands clapped together. Then heavy footsteps walking away.

The ding-dang rotters! They were betting on the lives of his mates. Gage's brain felt about to boil out of his head. He tensed, ready to spring out of the hold and charge at the men.

A tiny hand flicked his ear. The urge to attack lessened as he remembered where he was, but his anger at the dirty slaggers remained.

"Sorry," he murmured to Clax. "I figgered you was tryin' to keep me from helping Wynd."

Clax chimed a sour note in his ear.

Gage put a finger to his lips. "I know. I know." Clax was right, he should make an effort to trust better. Clax had just saved him from giving himself up to the brutal crew. Twice, if anyone was counting. And he and Clax had made a pact hadn't they? As he had with Wynd, he supposed. His face warmed. That was another pact he hadn't really trusted. If their aims weren't trued up, would she still be trying to help him?

There were too many thoughts in his head. Too many 'why fors' and 'what ifs.' He hadn't the time for all these niggling worries. He shook his head clear and pressed up on the hatch again. This time, it budged.

Chapter Thirty-Four
Not Quite Paradise

Wynd climbed up the ship's ladder, taking it slow and hoping the delay would give Gage the time he needed to reach the small boat and get it into the water. She gripped the rungs as if afraid—not a difficult thing to do, since her heart pounded inside her like a steam hammer—and let her feet stumble. Below her, Nobs and the other streeters crowded together, staring up at the bright expanse of sky visible through the open hatch.

"Oy, hurry it up. We ain't got all season." A burly man with a scraggly face full of whiskers and a shiny bald pate stood on the deck peering down at them. His red slash of a mouth was filled with black spittle from the nasty wad of tobacco stuffed inside his lower lip. His bitter breath wafted down into the hold. Wynd held her breath as she climbed the rest of the way up. Once on deck, she gulped in a lungful of clean air.

As the others climbed out of the hold, blinking

against the brightness after their time in the dark, Wynd's eyes finally adjusted. She gasped at the bright green vision that had materialized across the azure blue water.

An island of lush trees and growing things.

Rocky cliffs rose on one side of the island. In the distance, at what looked to be the center of the island, a huge mountain towered over everything.

"Welcome to my little patch of paradise."

Wynd spun around at the sound of the Captain's nasally voice. Nobs and the others huddled around her, gaping at the brilliant greenery as she had.

He crossed the deck to stand at the rail and stare across the water at the emerald island. "Lovely, isn't it?" He turned back to her, tugging at his lacy cuffs, adjusting them so they hung just so from the ends of his velvet sleeves. The crimson feathers in his jeweled and beribboned hat perfectly matched his fine coat.

Wynd's ire rose. The cost of his clothes could feed the entire Dartlings crew for a half-year. And here he was kidnapping them and hauling them off to this faraway place. But for what? She gazed back across at the island where frothy waves washed against sugar white beaches and green, green, green grew as far as the eye could see.

"I see you like it. Good. Good. It will be your new home, after all." The right side of the Captain's mouth quirked up in a sneery half-smile. "For as long as you last."

Chapter Thirty-Five
Change of Plans

Gage ducked behind a barrel and waited as Clax scouted the next leg of his path. According to Clax, he was half-way there. But it was taking forever what with having to duck and dodge out of sight each time another of the crew appeared hauling ropes or shifting cargo. He hadn't planned for all the activity. Seemed the entire crew was on deck and moving about.

Across the way, the last of the streeters were climbing out of the hold. Gage had watched as Tups emerged, followed by Nobs. When the Captain had stepped out of his cabin all dressed in his fine flippery-frippery, his bright red coat shone in the sun against the green of the island.

The island was like something from a dream. The dream that danced in his head at night. The dream his mother had woven for him of a fine wondrous place where sweet fruits grew wild and plentiful and the water ran clear and pure. And the air so clean...

He forced himself to pull his eyes away. He hadn't the time to admire it. Clax was already winging back, and Gage had work to do.

But even before the fairy settled onto his outstretched hand, he knew his luck had run out, or rather his bad luck, what seemed never-ending, was still with him.

Even with the difficulty Gage had understanding Clax, it didn't take long before he understood the problem.

No nearby dock.

Nor pier.

And the smugglers were already offloading the small boats for use in ferrying the prisoners and themselves across to the glistening beach. There would be no way for Gage to steal one without being seen.

"Change of plan, then." Gage chewed the inside of his cheek, deep in thought.

***

Wynd forced herself not to react at the bright flash of metal and wings that flitted over the Captain's head and landed as soft as a butterfly on his fancy hat.

Nobs opened his mouth, but Wynd pretended to lose her balance and jostled him with her elbow. "Ssshhhh," she hissed.

Nobs froze. He wiped his sleeve across his face, then turned his gaze away from Clax. Along with the rest of the streeters, he stared out at the emerald island that gleamed across the water.

Clax, perched upon the Captain's feather-festooned hat, wiggled its hands and arms at Wynd in some sort of strange pattern. She tried to decipher the clockwork's odd gestures, but she just couldn't make her brain make sense of what Clax was doing.

First the fairy waggled a finger at her, then made a sort of sweeping gesture followed by, well, to be honest, Wynd had no idea.

At the same time, the Captain was droning on about the island, its mysteries and its treasure trove of...

Finally, Clax stuck out its upturned hands and shrugged.

Wynd started to shake her head... *Wait, what?*

"Excuse me," Wynd said. "Did you say there's a source of power that doesn't require steam? Or wood? Or even coal?"

Clax shook its head no and started the whole process of gesturing over again, but Wynd was no longer paying the clockwork any mind. Her full attention was now on the Captain and what he was saying.

"Well, if you must know, it wasn't so much my discovery," he drawled. "But I daresay as I am the one to determine that the methods being used to extract it were nothing short of cumbersome. Not to mention, unnecessarily time consuming and tedious." He tugged at his lacy cuffs and brushed a bit of nothing from his sleeve.

All the while, Clax continued to wave and signal from atop his hat.

"And we're here to what?"

"Are you dim, girl? Has the witty vermin gone soft in the head? Tsk, tsk, tsk." He shook his head as he spoke.

Atop his hat, Clax grabbed a handful of plumes and hung on as his shaking head threatened to send the clockwork spinning.

"As I told you"—he raised one thick black eyebrow and stared at Wynd—"you'll be gathering my valuable resource for me."

"But why us?" Wynd understood the Captain needed laborers, but why a bunch of kids? Why not just round up some more criminals for the work?

"Hah, not so bright after all," Shields piped up. "It's on account of the gasses, ain't it?" He looked pleased with himself, but the Captain raised a finger into the air and the smile fell from Shields's face.

"What," the Captain said, "have I told you about interrupting?"

"Sorry, Cap'n."

The Captain dropped his finger and flourished his hand, palm up, and gave Shields a look of impatient expectation.

Shields squinted his eyes shut, then slapped himself hard across his face.

The resounding slap drew everyone's attention.

Even Clax froze.

Wynd stared round-eyed at the man.

"Now, don't make me have to school you again," the Captain said.

"Aye, Cap'n," Shields raised his hand up to cradle his reddened cheek.

"Now, where were we...?"

Shields opened his mouth, but a side-eye from the Captain made him shut it again.

"Ready the boats!" someone called out.

A flinch flashed across Shields's face. "Order, Cap'n?"

The Captain nodded, his fine plumery flagging with the motion. "Ah, yes. Thank you, Shields. As for you"—he flourished a finger at Wynd—"well, you'll learn soon enough."

Clax smacked a hand to its head in frustration and flew off.

"Boats?" Wynd repeated.

A sudden commotion arose on the back end of the ship. Shouts and splashes and the pounding of feet across the deck.

"What the devil? Shields!?!"

"Aye, Cap'n? I mean, I shall see to the ruckus forthwith, Cap'n." He rushed toward the chaos. "Come along, you," he shot the words over his shoulder at the crewmen standing watch over the streeters.

"But wha—" started one of the men.

"They ain't goin' nowheres," said the other, pushing up his sleeves and balling up his fists, "and I'm overdue for some exercises."

Wynd glanced behind her at the others. They stood huddled together wide-eyed.

"Why is it that I cannot enjoy a single smooth excursion?" The Captain pinched his nose between a thumb and forefinger.

Wynd rocked onto the balls of her feet. Part of her prepared to flee, another part gulped back fear.

"We should rename this ship the *None-in-a-Row*." The Captain put his fists on his hips and leaned forward, his feathery plumes threatening to fall into Wynd's face.

Behind her, the others shuffled their feet in nervous anticipation, waiting for her to give them the signal. But the noise from the small boats mixed with the sight of the wide wet expanse and the way the Captain's long fingers rested so close to the hilt of his narrow sword sent shivers running through her brain. It made it hard to think.

Finally, Nobs poked a bony finger into her back, making her jump and the word leaped from her mouth. "Skitter!"

The streeters scattered like mice. And Wynd sprang after them without looking back, hoping the Captain hadn't drawn his sword to come after them.

When she reached the ship's stern where the small boats had been made ready to drop overboard, she stopped and ducked just in time. A meaty arm swiped past her and just missed connecting with Nobs's skinny shoulders.

It was the most chaotic scuffle Wynd had ever seen, and she'd seen plenty since finding herself out on the streets with her brothers. Even more after she'd risen to lead the Dartlings gang.

But those were planned turf battles, designed to decide who owned what blocks. There were always some kind of tactics behind the way each gang attacked and counterattacked. This was just a bunch of angry men chasing a handful of streeters around the ship's deck.

The streeters had no plan, except to get to the boat that Gage had been planning to steal. But the few boats that were already in the water were all manned by smugglers. And where was Gage?

The sound of crowing overhead made her look up. High above, Gage clung below the crow's nest, loudly taunting the burly men who climbed up after him. But each time one of the smugglers got close, they found themselves harassed by a glittering stinging insect.

Clax zipped in and out, stabbing and slashing with its tiny sword. The men grabbed for their ears and tried to cover their faces, swatting wildly at their tormentor. But Clax was too fast for them, flitting in and out so fast it could hardly be seen, much less caught.

Men flailed, lost their footing and got tangled in the ropes. One man hung upside down, his face as red as the Captain's velvet coat.

"Wynd, look out," Gage shouted down at her.

She dodged just in time to escape Shields, who had tried to grab her. He stumbled forward, arms gripping air.

Wynd ran to the side of the ship and stopped. Her

heart swam up into her throat. Two of the streeters had jumped overboard and were paddling away from the ship. But the smugglers in one of the small boats were already closing in on them. And Wynd couldn't even swim. What was she supposed to do, now? She thought of Micah and Jasp. How even now they might be starving on the island, being driven to gather the Captain's precious rotted ore.

She had to do this. *Had to.*

She forced herself to grab the railing and started to climb. But before she managed to make it over the side, something sharp and shiny sliced through the sleeve of her shirt. The point of a sword hovered near her face.

"Ah, ah, ah."

She froze.

"Must I do everything my own self?" The Captain drawled, as he stepped up beside her and pointed the tip of his sword at her throat. "Come down now," he shouted up at Gage. "Or I'm afraid I'll have to make an example of your friend here."

Chapter Thirty-Six
Walking the Plank

"Change of plan?" Wynd scowled at Gage.

"Well, I tried to warn you."

"Right. Sending Clax to dance on the Captain's hat. So helpful. No wait. It wasn't."

From inside Gage's shirt pocket, Clax jangled an angry note.

"Don't blame Clax. It did its best. Asides, it's all we had time for, under the circumspection, weren't it?"

"You mean circumstances," Wynd grumbled.

"That's right," Gage said, "You're always right. We're standing at the end of a plank with nought but the wide ocean below with a gang o' smugglers ready to do us to our deaths, but you'll be right, won't ya?"

"And you always come up with the worst plans," Wynd groused. "Let's hop on board a big leaky tub full of smugglers. That's the ticket." She trembled beside him at the end of the long plank that stretched out over the deep water. Her angry words failed to mask the fear he saw in her eyes.

Something splashed in the waves beneath them and Wynd looked down. Her face turned an altogether pale shade of fright. Gage dared to look down and froze. His brain spun in circles more frantic than the mechanical beast that swam below them.

"Now, then. You two lardyballs hold that plank steady!" Shields ordered the sailors holding the other end of the board. "I'll be back in a spurt."

Shields suddenly disappeared and, a moment later, reemerged on deck carrying a long heavy cylinder shape. Gage realized with a start that it was the weapon he'd seen the Captain—who he was now sure had been Hannigan's dark-of-the-night customer—fire into the dousing barrel, sending a spray of splinters and water across the shop.

Gage's knees wanted to buckle. He couldn't decide which would be worse. If Shields were to shoot them with that blaster, or if the thing thrashing beneath them chomped them up.

"Shields?"

"Aye, Cap'n." Shields jiggled the levers and cranked the knobs on the sides of the weapon.

"Shields." The Captain leaned forward in his chair.

"Not to worry. I'll have it primed and ready in a moment."

"Shields! Leave off."

Shields looked up, blinking in confusion. "But Cap'n, you said as if *it* were to show itself uncontained and unexpected-like to fetch the bomblaster and have at."

"But right now, it's useful to us, isn't it?" He spoke calmly, though he stayed well away from the ship's rails, sitting tensed in the chair bolted to the deck. His knuckles turned white from the way he gripped the armrests.

"It is?" Shields tilted his head. "But..."

"They tried to escape. They caused an exceptional ruckus, yes?"

"Aye..."

"And their unacceptable troublemaking escapade has earned them a fitting punishment." He waved at Gage and Wynd. "I have decided, however, that they will be much more valuable as dinner time entertainment for the crew than as miners."

"But it's not anywhere near dinner time," Shields pointed out.

"Not dinner time for you, Shields. For IT!" The Captain pointed a shaky finger over the side of the ship where the metal beast jumped from the water and splashed down, glinting in the bright sunlight.

Gage hadn't gotten a solid look at it at first, but he saw now that what swam beneath them was the hugest crocodilly he'd had ever seen. Not that he'd ever actually seen one before. And not that this one looked like it *should* be alive, all made of metal as it was. But any rate it was huger than he imagined a real one might be.

Below him the creature ground its metal teeth. The smack of an impatient tail on the waves splashed a torrent of salty water to splatter over them and pool at their feet.

"Clax..." Gage patted his pocket. "You best head off to the island. No sense in all of us ending up in the belly of..." He paused. Did something like that even have a belly?

The rest of the streeters, including Nobs, had been pulled from the water and stood dripping on the deck, forced to watch what Shields called "a lesson in the matter of behaviors appropriate to their station."

The ship's crew rushed over and gathered along the rail to watch. "Ooh, looky there," one said. "The beastie's gettin' restless."

A bit farther along the rail two of the crew exchanged coins.

"One bite for each of 'em," said one.

"Naw," said the other, "that girl's a tall un. I 'spect it'll take two."

Shields stepped up to the plank, which was held in place by two brawny crewmembers. One of them was the man who had been dangling upside down from the rigging a short time ago. He glared at Gage with narrowed eyes. "Still like to know what the whatsit was what stung me," the smuggler muttered to the man beside him.

Shields reached down and swatted the man atop his head. "You'll be mindful of the nature of the serious business at hand to which we are engaging," he told the man. "By which I mean, shut yer yap."

The smuggler jerked away and the plank wobbled. Wynd yelped, squeezed her eyes shut and gripped Gage's shirt as the two of them nearly lost their balance.

"Hold the plank steady." Shields did a jig-step to regain his own balance.

The smuggler clapped his hands tight on the board and stared even more dagger-like at Gage.

From his seat on the deck, the Captain flourished a ruffled hand. "Get on with it, Shields. We haven't got all day. Well, actually"—he cocked his head to the side in thought—"we do, but I'd rather not spend it all on this bothersome nonsense."

"You heard the Cap'n"—Shields flicked his hands at them—"go on now. Let's not belay the final act."

Gage and Wynd stood frozen to the spot.

"Come on, now," Shields hissed at them, "Don't make me look bad in front of the Cap'n." He stomped his foot to shake them loose.

Neither of them budged.

"Are we there, yet?" the Captain asked with a bored look.

Shields glanced over his shoulder at the Captain. "Just savoring the moment, Cap'n. Providing a bit of extra entertainment for the men." He turned back to Gage and Wynd. "It's all the same ending for you, my pets. Whether you take the leap of your own accord, or opt for a skewering." He drew his sword, pointed the tip at Gage's head, and took a step forward.

Chapter Thirty-Seven
A Leap of Faith

"Sorry, Wynd." Gage's chest hurt. He thought about all the people he had failed. First his mother. Then his missing mates. Now Nobs and Wynd. If he jumped now, maybe he could choke the stupid mechanical monster that swam below. Maybe Wynd and his mates would survive. Maybe, if he caused a big enough distraction, they'd even find a way to escape. He gulped down his rising fear and whispered to Wynd, "When I say 'go,' run up the plank to the ship. And if worse comes to worst, remember, paddle like a dog."

"What?"

"Oy!" he shouted at the Captain and his crew of mangey smugglers. "You want a show? Well, here you go, then." He opened his pocket and nudged Clax out into the air behind the flap of his jacket, then gritted his teeth and prepared to jump. "Here. I..." Wynd froze. "Go!" Gage shouted and jumped as high into the air as he could, preparing to bounce off the end of the plank and somersault into the water below.

Wynd started to run. Something rushed by overhead. Gage ducked and, with a whir and a whoosh, Wind was gone.

Overhead, a wobbly-propellered flying machine swerved and banked, returning for another rescue attempt. "Jump!" shouted the pilot, a dark-haired girl with long braids. Her cheeks were reddened by the sun and wind. She tossed down a narrow rope-and-stave ladder for Gage to grab, but just then the croc leaped high into the air and caught Gage across the back of his leg with the tip of its hard tail. Gage's leg buckled. Pain seared his knee. With a yelp, he fell sideways, fingertips just missing the handhold the girl had extended.

"Hey, you dumb ticker," Wynd shouted. "I'm tastier." She dangled beneath another flyer, the grinning pilot still gripping her by one arm as they swooped down close to the water to distract the beast.

The smugglers hooted their encouragement, but their cheers died down as the lashing croc swung its tail hard against the side of the ship. "Shields!" the Captain's voice rose over the din. "Do something?"

The girl in the machine swerved back toward Gage. "Jump!" she yelled down to him. "Lufter has your friend."

"But our mates..."

"We only have room for two," Lufter hollered, buzzing the croc and whipping it into a frenzy. "And you're the two most in need."

The smugglers jeered, shaking their fists. The two men holding the plank still hadn't let go, but Shields jumped off the end and swatted them on their heads. Gage didn't have time to blink. The girl swerved back overhead and dipped down until the ladder was within reach. He grabbed onto the lowest rung and was lifted up just as the plank dropped from beneath him. His sudden weight dragged the flyer down toward the water. The croc's clacking metal jaws just missed removing his leg, but the jagged teeth caught hold of the heel of his shoe.

The buzz and whir of the flyer's propeller grew as the machine worked double, then triple power. The grinding gears ratcheted up till they screeched like an angry fishmonger. Gage felt like a knotted rope in a tug of war. His fingers clutched the handle of the machine as the mechanical beast clung to his boot, dragging him and the machine down toward the sloshing sea. His damp hands began to slip, his fingers pulling away from the handle. He was sure to be ripped in two or pulled from the flying machine and into the monstrous jaws of the mechanical horror. Then, the crock's teeth sliced through the heel of his worn boot and tore the sole away. The monster fell back into the water with a loud metallic slap and splash.

The flying machine leaped into the air, yanking Gage with it. Cold air whooshed across the bottom of his foot, and he tightened his grip on the handhold.

"Whooo-hoo-hoooo!" the girl pilot hollered. Her braids whipped in the wind, her eyes lighting up behind the thick goggles she wore.

Gage swung himself up to get a better hold, looping one arm over the metal bar and let relief roll over himself. Then he looked down. "What about our mates?"

Below them, the smugglers carried on as if someone had stolen their teeth, hopping up and down on the deck of the ship and raising angry fists into the air. Huddled to one side, the rest of the streeters watched them fly off.

"We can't take everyone with only two flyers." The

pilot shifted the wing flaps and lifted them higher.

"Then, take me back!" Gage shouted. "I can't leave them."

"Can't do it. Won't do it," she responded. "Have to find another way."

"I'll go back myself." Gage prepared to let go.

"Wouldn't." She pointed back toward the ship.

The croc continued to slam itself against the ship's hull, and a circle of sharp fins closed in, swishing back and forth with deadly grace. "Sharks!" Gage shouted. "There are sharks?" He tightened his grip as his belly fell through his feet. If the croc hadn't swallowed him whole, the sharks would have fought over any remains. And if he'd let go just now...

"Sea-kelpies!" Gage's rescuer shouted. "That should keep those filthy nabbers put for a while." She laughed, then let out another round of yodeling bellows. The other pilot responded in kind and they swept away above the thick greenery of the jungle.

They flew just above the tops of the lush trees, the chug and swish of the flying contraptions echoing over the dark-green jungle below, and up toward a tall peak that jutted up above everything else.

As they drew nearer, Gage began to make out what appeared to be doors and windows. A small city was carved into the side of the mountain with ladders and rope bridges that hung and stretched at dizzying angles from one ledge to another, connecting a number of stone houses together.

"What's that?" Gage shouted up to his rescuer to be heard over the noise of the sputtering engine and the clanking of metal cogs against one another.

"Home." Her voice held a strange sadness when she said it, but Gage could only stare in wonder at the height of the mountain and the drop from the lowest ledge into the dark shadows of the jungle below.

The wall of the cliff loomed ahead. "Shouldn't we be going higher?" Gage asked, trying to keep his voice from cracking.

Something sharp poked him in the chest and Clax buzzed inside his pocket.

"How'd you get back in there?" Gage asked, pulling open his jacket.

Clax pulled itself up far enough to peer out. It pointed at the cliff face and let out a series of sour notes.

"We're going to crash."

"Looks like it, doesn't it?" The pilot let out another peal of laughter.

Gage cringed.

Clax zipped out in an angry flash of red and flew into the pilot's face.

"Ahhh!" the girl shouted, raising one hand from the controls to swat at the fairy. "Get it off me. It's going to make us lose control."

"It's only trying to keep us from crashing."

"Stupid bug!" The pilot veered left and right, trying to shake Clax off, but the little metal creature was fast and determined.

Gage was tossed about like a raggedy doll being flung around by a frantic child. "Clax!" he yelled. "Layoff, afore I get drop-splattered."

Clax turned brighter red and dropped back, grabbing hold of Gage's collar, and clung on as the pilot regained control of her flyer. "That's better," the girl called. "Now, buckle up, we're coming in fast. I aim to beat Lufter this time"

Gage scrunched his eyes shut, but he couldn't take it. One eye peeled open just enough to see the face of the cliff coming up fast.

Chapter Thirty-Eight
Helping Hands

"Woo-hoo!" The other pilot swooped in, dropping his flyer out of the sky right in front of the one Gage clung to, and flew right for the cliff. Gage clenched his muscles, bracing for the impact. Then, with a rumble, a section of the cliffside slid away, opening into a wide space. The pilot eased back on his controls and dropped his flyer, landing gently onto the floor of a large room filled with all manner of contraptions. Wynd leaped down from her perch on the flyer's ladder as Gage and his pilot settled to the floor just behind them.

"Beat you, again!" The young man gloated as he turned knobs and flipped switches, shutting down the machine's power. It let out a low whistle, huffed out a final wheeze, and went silent. Then he undid the straps that held him secure in the seat and leaped out.

"Only because I was distracted." Gage's rescuer shut down her own machine, then swatted at a buzzing Clax, who jangled loudly before retreating back onto Gage's shoulder.

Wynd wobbled unsteadily, staring around in wonder at the strange equipment stored along the edges of the large room. "What is this? And who are you?"

"You're welcome." The girl undid the chin strap of her leather helmet, shaking her head and swinging her dark braids over her shoulders so they cascaded down her back.

Lufter shook his head and flipped a thumb in the girl's direction. "What she said." He gripped the cross piece of his flying machine and raised the front end, tilting it till it leaned back on a set of wheels on the back end. Then he pushed it into a space beside a rack filled with tools. "Needs a throttle adjustment." He settled the machine into place and ran his hand along the row of tools until his fingers closed on a long-handled one with a flat end.

The girl rolled her eyes. "Of course, it does. Or you would have beaten me even without the distraction. Right?"

"Exactly." He began tinkering with the machine, seeming to forget that anyone else was there.

Clax stood on Gage's shoulder and jangled as loud as possible. Gage's face turned bright red. "No, it's not." The fairy pinched his ear then buzzed to the top of the highest shelf and landed with an angry thud.

"Ow!" Gage rubbed his ear. Then he held out his hand to the girl. "I'm Gage."

Clax kicked at a tin of spare parts, knocking them to the floor in a crashing clatter, then crossed its arms and turned its back on all of them.

The girl eyed Gage's hand for a moment, then crossed her arms and narrowed her eyes. "You can call me Quill."

Lufter snorted.

"Thought you were going to fix that machine," Quill said.

"Oh, I am." He chuckled. "And next time I'll beat you by three lengths instead of two. *Quill.*"

"Right." She rolled her eyes. "So, you're Gage." She tilted her head to the side. "And you're...?"

"Both ought to be croc bait right about now," Lufter muttered.

"Sorry. My name is Wynd. And thank you for saving us from that monster."

"Machine," Quill corrected her. "My best invention." She turned to stare out the wide opening toward the distant ship. "Or should have been."

Wynd's mouth fell open. "You made that...that thing?"

"That *thing* was our best plan for keeping our people safe," Lufter interjected.

"But something went wrong," Quill whispered. "The smugglers got hold of it. And now it's become our biggest threat."

"Threat?"

"The smugglers are using it against us." Lufter tapped at a metal valve with a small brass hammer. "At least, it's always around when they are."

"We can't fish. We can't gather our crops." Quill shook her head. "Every time we send out a foraging party, someone disappears."

"Like my...my mates," Wynd said.

"And mine," Gage added. "They's all the family we got."

"Sounds like we've all lost someone." Lufter wiped his greasy hands on a rag.

"Sounds to me like we've got a common enemy," Quill said. "So, what are we going to do about it?"

Clax crept to the edge of the shelf and stared down, wing tips flickering in agitation.

"And who's your spying little friend?" Quill flicked her eyes up at Clax. "Don't think I didn't notice you up there plotting," she called out.

"Clax is a mech—" Wynd started, but Gage cut her off.

"Clax hain't a spy," he said. "Clax is an ally."

Clax flashed blue and blew raspberries at Wynd.

"You've a clockwork bug that's an ally?" Lufter's face lit up. He set aside his tools and stepped closer to the shelf where Clax was standing.

Clax flashed red and let out a noisy jangle.

"Don't call it that," Gage warned.

"Yeah. Not unless you want your ears pierced," Wynd said.

"Come on down, little one," Lufter called. "Let's have a look at you."

Clax's chin went up, nose pointed to the ceiling.

"I'm not going to hurt you." He held out his hand. "How about you come down and say hello?"

Clax turned and gave a wing flick, but stayed on the shelf.

"That one doesn't trust anyone," Wynd said with a huff. "Except him." She pointed at Gage.

"Guess I'm just trustworthy." He gave her a smug grin.

"Don't start that up again."

Gage held up his hands in surrender. "Fine." He turned away. "But the pudding proves it."

"I heard that," Wynd said. "And it's the proof is in the pudding."

"Exactly." Gage smirked.

"I give up," she said.

Lufter and Quill shook their heads.

"Fine." Quill jerked her head in Clax's direction. "What are you and your ally doing on our island?"

"Come to rescue our mates," Gage told her.

"Rescue, eh?" Lufter shook his head. "They're as

good as goners, if those smugglers have got their grips on them."

Wynd scowled. "That's what you say."

"That's what I *know*," Lufter said. "Unless you have better allies than a clockwork bug."

Clax jangled a harsh note and prepared to leap down from the shelf, but Gage waved the clockwork back. "He's just trying to get a rise out of you, Clax."

"Worth a try to get a closer look." Lufter shrugged.

Clax clanged a harrumph and sat on the edge of the shelf.

"He's right at any rate," Quill told them. "If your friends are here and the smugglers brought them, they'll be working them in the crater. And the way they're dredging out the ore, with no precautions, they won't last long in there."

"What do you mean no precautions?" Wynd's face filled with worry.

"What she means," Lufter chimed in, "is that the ore they're dredging from the core isn't safe to just dig up. It has to be gentled out of the earth. The way they're doing it, they might as well be spraying poison into the air and then sucking in big gulps of it."

"He's right," Quill agreed. "Bad enough in there when the gathering is done right, but without precautions? No one should be in there without a solid-built filtration mask, gathering kit, triple-layered gloves—"

"No." Gage shook his head. "I say we're going to rescue them." He pointed his thumb at his chest. "No Lostun left back."

"Nor Dartling," Wynd added, her jaw set.

Quill and Lufter raised their eyebrows in unison.

"Think we haven't tried to rid our island of that scummy gang of muckrakers?" Lufter tossed the rag onto a workbench. "They're destroying our home. It's not just the air they're poisoning."

Quill nodded. "What's sifting out into the water is worse. You saw what it's done to the sea-kelpies."

"Sea-kelpies?" Wynd asked. "Is that what those creatures were circling the ship?"

"*Those creatures* used to be friendly," Quill grumbled. "*Those creatures* used to live in peace with us."

"We traded with them." Lufter said. "We were... allies." He jutted his chin up at Clax.

"Before the smugglers discovered the ore on our island."

"Before they came in numbers too large to repel and seized the crater."

"We would have shared," Quill said. "We tried to tell them, tried to show them the way to gather the ore without destroying our island."

"We told them about the dangers."

"But they wouldn't listen."

"Because they're greedy."

"They have no patience."

"They wrecked our way of life," they finished together.

"Then help us," Gage said. "You and us. We can be allies."

"We can work together," Wynd added. "Rescue our family...our friends...and send every one of those rotten scoundrels back where they came from."

Quill and Lufter looked at one another.

"Yes," said Quill.

"No," Lufter blurted.

Quill smirked. "Beat you."

"Doesn't matter." Lufter crossed his arms. "Too dangerous."

"We have to help," Quill insisted.

"Why?" Lufter asked.

"Because it's my fault." Quill began to shake.

"They're using the croc to keep the workers in line. The croc is my monster. I made it. I need to stop it."

Lufter started to argue, then stopped. He uncrossed his arms and reached over to pat Quill's shoulder. "Okay, okay." He turned to Gage and Wynd. "We'll help," he told them. "But it won't be easy."

Chapter Thirty-Nine
Not So Much

"How many of the islanders will help us?" Wynd asked.

"None," Lufter said.

"What?" Gage's mouth fell open. "But—"

"They're gone," Quill cut him off. "Well, mostly." She glanced over at Lufter, but he was busy searching the shelves for something.

"Mostly?" Wynd let hope seep into her question.

Quill frowned.

"Nope," Lufter called over his shoulder. "Not on your life."

Quill waved him off. "A few of the elders refused to leave. Including our Gran."

"Can they help?" Gage asked.

"No." Lufter left off searching the shelves and turned to them.

"Why not?" Gage frowned.

"First off, because, nope. And second, because, nope, nuh-uh." Lufter ticked off on his fingers and shook his head.

"Oh, stop being so...dramatic. And vague." Quill told him. "Lufter doesn't want, um, them to know."

"That we're planning to fix things?" Gage asked.

"No." Quill glanced over at Lufter. "That we're still here. We were supposed to leave with the rest. Only we hid and snuck back into the hangar, instead. Only flew out to do a sweep when we saw the ship."

Lufter glared back at her. "Lucky for you," he told Gage and Wynd. "And your clockwork...friend." He jerked his thumb in the direction of Clax.

"If you didn't really want to help us before, that means you didn't stick around to do anything about the smugglers. So, why did you bother to stay?" Gage asked, his eyes narrowed in suspicion.

Quill and Lufter looked at one another, but neither of them said anything.

"Anyway, they don't know we're here," Quill said, finally.

"And they're not going to find out from me," Lufter huffed.

"But they might need to know," Quill said. "If things go wrong..."

"Things can't go wrong," Lufter insisted. "We have to make sure."

"And how are we going to do that?" Wynd asked.

"Don't know yet," Lufter said. "Still figuring."

Chapter Forty
Mapping Things Out

"What's that bit there?" Wynd stood in front of the long table where Lufter and Quill had arranged tools and machine parts to represent the landmarks of the island. A line of wrenches represented the cliff wall surrounding the village. A box of bolts was the hangar they were in. And a stack of sharp-toothed cogs sat at the farthest edge.

"Lagoon Rock," Lufter said as he stacked them. "Sharp teeth like the sea-kelpies."

Quill chewed her lip. "My fault, too."

"Not." Lufter frowned at her. "You didn't tell."

"Might as well have." Her shoulders sagged.

"Didn't tell what?" Gage asked.

"About the ore." Lufter twirled a tool in his fingers. His hands seemed to always be moving, like he couldn't bear to be still, while Quill could become as still as a tree.

"Maybe you better tell us more about this ore the smugglers want," Gage said.

"It was a secret kept on the island for a long, long time." Quill sighed.

"Used it for heating and to light up the dark nights."

"Like coal?"

"Yes." Lufter said at the same time Quill said, "No."

"Which is it?" Wynd demanded.

Lufter shrugged. "Both. Kinda."

Quill frowned. "Well, it does make power."

"So, it can make steam from water?" Gage asked.

"Sure." Lufter nodded. "But mostly why would you?"

"To make things work, like engines and stuff." Gage waved at the flying machines parked nearby.

Lufter laughed. "You can use it to generate power. You don't have to make steam with it, though." He pointed at Clax "You don't see your little pet needing water or releasing steam from any valves, do you?"

Clax blazed red and let out the loudest jangle yet.

"Wouldn't call Clax a pet, if I was you." Gage warned, but his gaze fell on the clockwork and his forehead wrinkled in thought. "But, now you mention it, Clax hain't really big enough for a boiler, is it?"

Clax turned its back and flew off to a corner of the room.

Wynd began to nod. "So, this volcano ore, it makes power but not by turning water into steam." She gazed off to where Clax sat sulking. "And it doesn't burn like coal, either. So, no smoke?"

"Exactly," Quill said.

"Then how does it work?" Gage asked.

"Once you add it together with some sand and salt crystals, all you need is just a few drops of seawater to get it going and poof!" Lufter slapped his hands together then yanked them apart like they'd been forced. "Energy."

"Clean energy," Quill said.

"Mostly."

"No smoke."

Lufter shrugged.

"Harnessed by our ancestors."

"The secret to mining it safely was passed down the generations."

"Then I made the croc." Quill shut her eyes and stood silent.

"Why?" Wynd asked.

"To protect us," Lufter told her.

Quill's eyes popped open. "But it didn't." Her words were angry and sharp like the edges of the stacked cogs.

"Not your fault," Lufter insisted. "You meant right."

"Best intentions?" Quill shook her head. "We're outnumbered. Out-knived. And they have the croc."

Wynd stepped between them. "But we're going to fix things, now."

"Yeah," said Gage. "We'll help set things right. And rescue our mates."

Clax chimed from the shelf.

"See?" Gage said. "Even Clax says so."

Clax chimed again and swooped down from the shelf to hover over the map. It flashed blue, then red, then blue again, chiming each time.

"I don't think that's what it's saying," Wynd said.

"Huh?" Gage looked up at the clockwork fairy. "What're you trying to tell us, Clax?"

It flashed faster and clanged louder, sounding like an alarm.

"Slow down," Gage said. "I can't understand what you're saying."

Clax dropped down to land on the stack of sharp cogs and tapped its foot while pointing down.

"Oh," Gage said. "You think you can convince

them?"

"Convince? Convince who of what?" Lufter asked.

"Clax thinks we should even the odds by recruiting the sea-kelpies."

"Too dangerous," Quill shook her head. "They're not friendly. Not anymore."

Lufter huffed. "They were barely civil before. Now?" He made a terrified face.

Clax flickered and chimed, pointing and waving.

"Well?" asked Wynd once Clax became silent.

"Clax says the kelpies might be angry about what's happened, and about the croc and all, but they must want the same thing we do. They want to get rid of the smugglers and for things to go back to the way they were. Clean water to swim in and all."

"How does Clax know that?" Quill asked.

"Because Clax is smart," Gage said. "And knows what it is to need allies."

Lufter rolled his eyes. "Why should we listen to a clockwork bug?"

"Oh, stop being like that," Quill told him. "You're just mad because you can't figure out how it works."

"Can so." Lufter made a face at her. "You know, too." He raised an eyebrow. "Here, catch." He tossed something across the room toward Clax.

The clockwork zipped across the space and grabbed onto the small shiny thing. It made a small tink when Clax caught it. It held the brassy disc up and shrugged. Then the disc began to glow.

Lufter smirked. "Told you."

Quill's eyebrows arched up. "Ooooh..."

"Ooooh?" Gage wrinkled his forehead. "What's that supposed to mean?"

"That your Clax is like our croc."

Clax jangled an ugly sound, made a swift pass over the table and dropped the bit of still-glowing metal onto it. Then flew back to stand on Gage's shoulder.

"What Clax said." Gage stuck his thumb at the fairy.

"Okay. Not exactly like the croc," Quill said.

"But made up of the same kind of stuff," Lufter insisted. "Someone with a finer hand than you made it." He eyed his sister.

"I wasn't going for subtle." She frowned. "The point is, they're both powered with ore."

"It's why the croc can swim." Lufter picked up the washer Clax had dropped and rubbed it between a thumb and forefinger. "And crunch things."

"It's why it can fly." Quill waved a hand at Clax. "And stab things."

"Oh." Wynd glanced at Clax in surprise. "I knew there was something...different."

Clax waggled its head in a mockery of Wynd.

Wynd rolled her eyes at the clockwork fairy. "I didn't say it was a *bad* different."

"There's a huge difference between the croc and Clax," Gage said.

"What's that?" Lufter asked.

"Clax is our ally. And an official Lostun." He crossed his arms. "Clax is family."

Chapter Forty-One
A Spark of an Idea

"Can't sneak up on 'em." Lufter shook his head.

"Why not?" Gage chewed his lip in frustration. Every single idea had got tossed out as soon as it was thought up.

"Way through the rocks is shifty." Lufter dropped a handful of gears and cogs, letting them scatter across the table. "Every time the volcano gets rumbly."

"Plus, lookouts." Quill pointed along the chain they had used to mark out the rim of the crater. She placed several bolts along the edge.

"And guards on the workers." Lufter added a few bolts to the middle of their makeshift map, beside a small group of washers. "They keep an eye out, now."

"Those are our mates?" Gage pointed at the washers. "Not very many of them."

"Not sure how many are left." Lufter shrugged. "Some got out last time we buzzed 'em."

"Some? How many?" Wynd asked.

"Not sure." Quill shrugged.

Wynd's shoulders drooped.

"But that's why they watch 'em closer, now," Lufter said.

"Even though, they keep bringing more," Quill added.

"How many were on the ship with you?" Lufter asked.

Wynd frowned. "Aside from us there were five."

"Six," Gage corrected her.

"Sure." She crossed her arms over her chest. "If you count your can't-be-trusted friend."

Gage crossed his own arms. "He's a Lostun. He counts."

"Fine," Wynd huffed. "Doesn't really matter, does it? Not if we don't know how many are still down there? So, how do we get down into that crater without being seen?"

"We don't." Lufter suddenly grinned.

"Right." Quill smiled back.

"What are you so happy about?" Gage asked.

"Can't sneak in, but you don't have to." Lufter said.

Quill smacked her forehead. "So simple."

"Right. All you gotta do is pretend to try." Quill nodded.

"And let yourselves get caught."

"What?!?" Wynd and Gage said at the same time.

"It could work," Quill said. "You go in like you're on your own and get caught."

"Then you send your ally, there, out to let us know you're in place." Lufter pointed at Clax. "We'll make a buzz run."

"A big distraction," Quill added.

"And you lead your friends out the way you went in."

"What if it doesn't work?" Wynd looked worried.

"If all else fails," Lufter said, "There's one last solution."

"No." Quill's lips drew into a straight line. "That's not a solution."

"Well, only as a last resort."

"What?" Wynd asked.

"There is one other way to shut down the ore gathering, if our plan fails."

"What's that?"

"We set off a sparker."

"A sparker?"

Lufter held up an egg-shaped object with a lever on the side of it.

"It's what we drop on those filthy smugglers when we buzz them."

"Oh, like fiery bombs?"

"They're not actually fire."

"Or bombs."

"They're igneum."

"The dirty bits of the ore."

"The stuff that's left after we separate the vulcanite bits."

"You mean the stuff you said was poisonous?"

"Not when you separate it out and set it off in a sparker." Lufter turned the metallic egg over in his hand. "When we pull the lever and drop 'em, they're more like, um, party favors."

"Big noise, lots of sparks." Quill nodded.

"More scary than dangerous."

"Unless you drop 'em in the ore fields."

"It would stop the pollutants from getting out," Lufter said.

"And destroy our only power source."

"Worth it."

"Not."

"Why not?" Wynd asked.

"Because it's too dangerous. And..." Quill's face grew pale.

"And what?" Wynd asked.

"It'd shut down your friend." Lufter pointed at Clax.

"If it's too close." Quill said.

"Completely." Lufter dragged a finger across his neck.

Clax jangled a fearful chime and turned bright red.

"Well, that's not gonna happen." Gage reached out his hand to Clax.

Chapter Forty-Two
Best Intentions

They were still arguing about it when a small door at the rear of the hangar flew open with a bang and a dark form filled the doorway. "You were told to leave," a gravelly voice said.

Clax started and zipped up into the rafters to hide in the shadows.

Gage and Wynd ducked behind some machinery in the corner.

Quill and Lufter froze.

"What have you got to say for yourselves?" The old woman who walked across the room to where they stood, was thin and wrinkled, her skin dark, like a sailor who'd been out to sea for years.

Lufter bowed his head. "We couldn't leave you, Gran."

Quill shook her head. "You're all we have, since—"

"I am your guardian." The old woman placed a fist to her heart. "And I am your elder. But do you listen to me?" She shook her head. "No. I have failed."

Quill rushed to her side. "No, Gran. You haven't failed. It's us. We..."

"We have a plan," Lufter blurted.

"No!" the old woman shouted. "No plan. No." She waved her hand in front of her as she spoke, as if she could brush away the words he'd spoken.

Quill took the woman's hands. "Yes, Gran. We have a plan. A way to make things right. But now, it's your turn to leave. Your turn to be safe."

Lufter nodded. "We're not little children anymore, Gran."

"Not little. But still children." She pulled her hands away from Quill.

"It's time for us to help."

"How? Like before?"

Quill looked as if she'd been slapped.

Lufter stepped between them. "That was not her fault." He glanced at Quill. "It was mine."

"Stop," Quill said. "That isn't true and you know it. I made—"

"You don't know..." Lufter turned to his sister. "No one knows...what I did. It was me. I let the croc out. I thought I had control, but..." His voice dropped. "I was wrong."

"What?" Quill stepped back. "All this time..."

"I was looking for a way to fix it," Lufter told her. "So, everyone could stop blaming you."

"So you could be the hero, again, you mean," Quill shouted.

Lufter hung his head. "So you wouldn't hate me."

Quill's anger turned to shock. "How could you think—"

"You both stop," Gran ordered. "You"—she pointed to Quill—"you made the beast for a good reason. And you"—she placed a gnarled hand on Lufter's shoulder, and a sad smile spread across her face. "You could never leave well enough alone. Not when it's made of gears." She turned her face to the shadows where Gage and Wynd were hiding. "And you two. Are you part of this plan?"

Gage and Wynd stepped forward. "How?"

"I am old," Gran said. "But I have good ears."

Gage stared at the old woman. Her eyes squinted nearly shut as she peered at him, but her face was alert. "I heard you breathing in the shadows. Loud as a snuffling boar."

"Oh," Gage said.

Gran pointed up at the corner of the room where Clax hid, still and silent. "Not sure what that is," Gran said. "But I know it doesn't breathe."

Clax's tiny wings buzzed in surprise.

"Clax is...a friend," Wynd said.

Gage gave Wynd a funny look.

She shrugged back at him. "An ally, anyway."

"Not much here to go against a pack of violent criminals," Gran said, her voice shaky. "You need to leave."

"No, Gran," Lufter and Quill said together. "We're staying."

The old woman's lips trembled and tears fell from her eyes. "I, too, thought we could stay. I had hoped the island would keep us. But..." She shook her gray head. "Our home is preparing to dispossess us. We are no longer welcome on this land. It is time to go." Her shoulders drooped. "For all of us."

Quill and Lufter mouthed words at one another behind her back.

"I know when you do that," Gran said.

Lufter rolled his eyes.

"And that."

"But, Gran—"

"I have spoken." Gran chopped the air with a hand. "Besides, we need your help to leave the island."

"But we have only the two working flyers." Quill

frowned. "We can't take more than one passenger each, and..."

Gran opened and closed her fingers and Quill stopped talking.

"We have one last trick in our bag," Gran said. "A last way off the island. But I need your help."

"Oh." Lufter said.

"You should go," Quill said.

"What?" Lufter stared at her in surprise.

"Gran needs help."

"But what about you?"

Quill waved at Gage and Wynd. "So do they."

"We need you both." Gran frowned. "And they should come with us."

"But what about our mates?" Gage asked.

"We can't go without them," Wynd said

"We have done all we can." Gran shook her head. "We have saved those we could."

"Saved?" Wynd asked, her words hopeful. "You managed to save some of the streeters? Was it two boys? One taller than me and thin with dark hair, the other just about this high?" She held her hand out at her waist.

Gran shook her head again. "Two girls, and one boy, this size." She gestured at chest level.

Wynd's hope left in a rush.

"Sorry," Lufter said. "Guess the ones you're looking for are still in the crater."

"But we gotta help Gran get everyone else off the island." Quill frowned.

"Fine," Wynd told them. "You go ahead. But we're staying."

Clax let out a loud jangle.

"She's right, Clax. We gotta stay."

Clax crossed its arms and glared at Wynd.

"Come, then," Gran waved at Quill and Lufter. "Plenty to do. Not much time." She turned and shuffled toward the door.

"The plan can still work," Quill whispered. "We'll drop you on the way, help Gran, then catch up to you."

Lufter held out the sparker to Gage. "Here."

He shook his head and refused to take it.

"Too dangerous," Quill warned.

Lufter shrugged. "What isn't, now?" He shoved the sparker into Gage's pocket. "Last resort, yeah? Just make sure your friend isn't nearby."

Gage glanced over at Clax and stiffened. The weight of the sparker in his pocket pulled at him. He couldn't bear to think about using it. Not even as a last resort.

Chapter Forty-Three
Unnatural Allies

The afternoon sun beat down as they hiked across the uneven ground, pushing their way through the lush green ferns and stepping around tall trees with long fronds.

Quill and Lufter had flown them down from the hangar. They'd dropped them off at the foot of the cliff and pointed them toward the crater, before heading off to help their gran. Clax scouted ahead, flying back every few minutes to let them know they were still heading in the right direction.

Finally, they reached the edge of the lush green space. The rising slope of the volcano's crater loomed before them.

"That's it, I guess." Gage wiped the sweat from his forehead with a sleeve.

"How should we do this?" Wynd asked.

Gage shrugged. "We can't just wander along the edge making a big ruckus till one of their lookouts spots us, I s'pose."

"Too obvious."

"Get as close as we can and make a bungle of it?"

"That's about as good as anything I can think of." Wynd sighed. "Won't be too hard to make a bungle of it once we start down the inside of that." She pointed at the sloping side of the crater.

They snuck from bushy fern to the next, ducking below the tufts of tall grassy plants. The sun had dropped low in the sky and they'd just started up the outside of the crater when something hissed from the thick vegetation.

They froze.

"Is it a snake?" Wynd whispered, afraid to move.

"Pssssst!" It hissed from right beside her and she jumped.

"Hahahahaha," Checks laughed, crashing out of the nearby brush.

"Not. Funny." Wynd balled up her fists.

"Yeah. It was." Checks doubled over with glee.

"Sshhhh." Gage shushed them. "Someone'll hear."

"I thought that was the point," Wynd grumbled.

"Not like this," Gage said. "How'd you get away, Checks?"

Checks waved a hand at Gage, working to catch his breath. "Hold on. Hold on. Gimme a tick."

"Yeah." Wynd's eyes narrowed in suspicion. "How *did* you get away?"

Checks stopped laughing. "One of them smugglers as was guarding all of us had a coughing fit from all the dust and fell right over." His face grew serious. "Took my chance."

"Did anyone else get away?" Wynd asked.

Checks glanced back at the crater. "Naw. None that I saw."

"So, you just high-tailed it out of there and left everyone else to fend for themselves?" Wynd spoke through gritted teeth.

"Oy. Wasn't nothing for one lone fella to do, now was there?" Checks held up his hands. "I was figgerin' ta go back. Soon as I noodled out a good plan."

"Like we're supposed to believe that." Wynd huffed.

"Hang on." Gage stepped between them. "We're allies, 'member?"

Wynd grumbled, but shrugged.

"Allies? Pah." Checks spit on the ground.

"Not just a liar and a betrayer," Wynd frowned. "Also, a disgusting coward."

"This what you've been doing when you was s'posed to be out working? Hullaballooing around with a Dartling?" Checks gave Gage a shove. "Talk about a be-traitor."

Gage steadied himself. "Not. And you're just lucky I was out doing what I been doing, which as a matter of fact hadn't been hubbaballooing."

Checks snickered. "Lucky, am I?"

"Come on, Gage. Let's leave this rotter to help himself."

"Rotter, is it? Not near as much a one as you and those twiddling mates a yours."

"I'll show you twiddling!" Wynd tried to push past Gage, but he stood his ground.

"We made a pact," he reminded her.

Checks smirked. "Hah. You made a pact with the likes a that?"

Gage rounded on him. "Yeah, I did. And hain't no one taking it back till we done what we set out to do."

"And what'sat?" Checks sneered.

"Work together, till all our mates is rescued," Gage told him. "And we may's well start with you."

"Me?" Checks started to laughed, but it turned into a cough. "Well, that's the dankdest, nicest, best thing you've ever done for me, Gage. But, as you can see, I hain't in need of a rescue."

"Good." Wynd grabbed Gage by the sleeve. "Then we'll just be on our way."

"What I mean is, I can help," Checks said.

"That's a great idea." Gage pulled out of Wynd's grip. "More grease makes for a smoother engine."

"I don't trust him." Wynd folded her arms across her chest. "Where'd he get that fancy bit of equipage?" She pointed at the heavy goggles slung around Checks's neck.

Checks frowned. "Not that I needs to explain to you, but I bumped it off'n a dirty smuggler." He narrowed his eyes at Wynd. "What makes you think we can trust *her*? Don't it seem fishy she'd be so willing to team up with the likes 'o you?" He cocked his head to one side. "I mean, yer not the most dependable type, yerself."

The cold truth of what Checks said numbed Gage down to his toes. The past rushed over him and crushed him beneath the dark remembrance. That day. If only he'd stayed close to home as his mother had asked. Instead, he'd gone out. And the coppers had come. Dragged her from the tiny room they'd called home. Accused her of crimes she'd had nothing to do with...

"Gage." Wynd nudged him with a bony elbow. "You okay?"

"Fine." Gage stared down at his feet, wishing the lie to be true.

"We need to get a move on."

"Where to?" Checks asked, his eyes glinting.

"Not your business," Wynd snapped.

Gage sucked in a ragged breath. "We're—"

Clax erupted in the air with a jangle.

Checks ducked and swatted at the fairy. "Get back!"

Wynd snickered. "He's afraid of Clax."

"He was just startled is all." Gage held out a hand

for Clax to land on.

"What is 'at?" Checks peered at the clockwork, eyes wide.

Gage's face warmed. He hadn't planned on Checks knowing about Clax. Leastways not till he'd figured out how Clax was going to help the Lostuns escape Landings. But here it was. They weren't in Landings anymore. And they'd need all the help they could get to save the rest of their mates. "Clax's a friend, and is going to help us rescue Nobs and them."

"Right. That bitty bit of a metal toy is goin'ta help." Checks smirked. "Still the big time storyteller, ain't ya?"

"Not a story. And Clax hain't a toy. Right, Clax?"

Clax jangled, turned blue, then flashed red.

"What's that bit about?"

"Hain't nothin'." Gage gave Clax a look. "Clax just gets funny 'round new people is all. Don't pay it no mind."

Clax jangled louder and buzzed overhead in a circle.

"Don't look like no never mind, to me."

Wynd narrowed her eyes at Checks. "Looks to me like Clax doesn't trust you anymore than I do."

"Hah. We'll see about that." Checks reached up and tried to grab Clax out of the air.

"Leave be," Gage shouted, swatting at his arm.

"Hey. What the..." Checks swung back and made a fist, then an instant later dropped his arm. "Whoa. Hold on now. Didn't realize it meant so much to ya, Gage." He put his hands up.

Gage scratched the side of his neck, then glared up at Checks. "Clax is pack. We made a swear."

Clax swooped down and landed on Gage's shoulder, feet spread, hands on hips, and gave a curt nod.

Checks started to say something, then seemed

to think better of it. "Whatever you say." He glanced over his shoulder. "But I think we'd best be gettin' on with whatever it is you've got planned, eh?"

Wynd frowned. "So, now you're in a hurry?"

Checks shrugged. "Smugglers to best, mates to save, an' all like that. Right, Gage?" He gave Gage a light punch on the shoulder.

"Right." Gage rubbed his shoulder in thought. Checks hadn't hit him hard. It had just been a friendly tap. But Gage couldn't remember Checks ever touching him any way but mean. Maybe things really were finally going to go their way. Maybe, there was hope.

Chapter Forty-Four
A Stunning Surprise

They climbed to the rim of the volcano and peered over the edge. With the sun already on its way down the sky, dark shadows filled the crater. Rough rocks of all sizes littered the pit. A cloudy haze filled the deep bowl, but despite the gloom, they could make out movement far below. The scrape of tools echoed off the rock walls, mixing into a scramble of rattling stones and clanking metal.

"There they are," Gage murmured.

"How d'ya know?" Checks asked, his voice too loud.

"Shhhhh," Wynd hushed him.

He rolled his eyes at her, but lowered his voice. "How d'ya know it's them, then?"

"Who else would it be?" Wynd rolled her eyes back at him.

Clax tinkled with laughter.

"Come on," Gage grumbled. "Could we all please just try to get on? Leastwise till we get our mates back?"

"Fine," Wynd huffed.

Checks smirked.

"Checks?" Gage urged.

"Oy, fine."

"Good, then make yourselves a sensation of hostelries, will ya?"

"You mean a cessation of hostilities," Wynd corrected him.

Checks laughed.

Gage eyed them both and set his jaw hard. "Just spit 'n' shake on it."

Wynd balled up her fists, tightening them till her knuckles popped. "As if."

Checks sneered. "Don't need to go all overboard on it, do we? How's about we just agree to not disagree? For now."

Gage eyed the steep slope before them. "Clax, you best scout ahead. We'll duck around and catch up below."

Clax hesitated, then jumped into the air and disappeared.

Checks stared after the clockwork, eyes glinting with wonder.

"Come on," Gage told them. "We need to get a move on."

They crept forward, picking their way across the rocky waste.

Gage stumbled on a patch of loose rocks and cursed under his breath. "Ding-dang these mismatched boots."

Wynd struggled behind him, her own scuffed-up shoes slipping on the uneven surface. "You're lucky to have boots at all. Or feet to wear them on for that matter. After that stunt on the ship."

"I know. I know. I just wish Quill could have found a matching pair that fit."

"I'd make you a new sole," Lufter had said, "but I'm not that kind of mender." So, Gage had had to make do. At least they'd been able to provide a few tools that might help them rescue the streeters along with some decent goggles and filter cloths. "You'll need them down in that pit," Quill had said. So, here they were, across the water, heading down into a pit, after all.

A dusty haze filled the pit. Unlike the bitter smoke of Landings, it floated in the air and glittered like sparkles where the sun caught it. But just like the smoke and smog of Landings, it made it hard to breathe and they covered their faces with the muzzy filter cloths Lufter and Quill had given them. Gage even went so far as to cut a jaggedy line down the middle of his and offered half to Checks. The Lostuns leader took it with nary a thank you, which Wynd found rude. Even as the head of the Dartlings, she'd managed to mind her manners, but she kept her lips zipped. Lostuns had their own rules. Every streeter pack did. And it was best not to expect otherwise. Nor to try and force one pack's rules on another.

They cut across an open space between tall boulders, slipping in and out of the shadows.

"You!" A voice behind them shouted.

They turned to see a snarling smuggler stomping his way toward them.

"What are you doing? Trying to sneak off, eh?" The smuggler drew out a long knife and pointed it at them.

"We weren't...wait, where's—" Wynd started, but Gage cut her off with an elbow in her ribs. He slid the sack of tools from his shoulder. She took the hint and shuffled around behind him, searching the rocks for Checks. The Lostuns' leader seemed to have melted away just as the smuggler showed up and she couldn't shake the feeling he was up to something. She slipped the pack off her shoulder, lowering it to the ground, hoping whatever Checks was doing was going to help.

"You weren't what? Trying to scarper off? Just got turned 'round, did'ja?" The smuggler scratched his scraggily beard and laughed. Then he coughed, a raspy gargling sound, and spat on the rocky ground. "Goin' the wrong way. Or, as I might have it now, the right way. If you get my meanin'." He stuck the point of his knife in Gage's face. "Go on. Turn 'round and get back ta work. We ain't got all day. Cap'n'll want to be leaving afore this here mountain rumbles its last. Lots to get done afore then."

Gage stepped toward the smuggler and lowered his head, letting the hair fall forward over his eyes. "Sorry, sir. It's just that, my, my sister...she's awful ill." He glanced back at Wynd. She hacked out a not very believable cough.

"Sick is it? Aye, we're all getting the draughts working in this pit." He reached out his hand and rapped against a black rock with his knuckles. "Pretty though it be."

"Yeah. Anyways, we were just looking for some, er, some clean water for her, um, her throat."

"Clean water?" The smuggler let out a harsh snort. "Not here. Not anymore. Them village folks told 'em, but, never mind—wait, how'd you get loose from them chains?" He narrowed his eyes at them. "You should be all hooked up to the others, nice and tidy like—"

The man's body jittered and his words cut off as he slumped to the ground, a dazed look in his eyes.

"What was that?" Wynd asked.

"I don't know," Gage said, just as a flicker of gold and silver dropped onto his shoulder.

Clax.

The clockwork fairy dusted its hands and jingled

lightly.

"Thanks, Clax," Gage said. "Not sure how you done it, but we're grateful."

"Weren't it." A shadow moved forward and held up a rock before dropping it on the ground with a thunk.

"Oh. Thanks, Checks." Gage nodded.

Wynd stared at him in surprise.

"Whatsamatter?" Checks smirked at her. "Thought I'd up an' scarpered off?"

Wynd eyed him with distrust. "Yes, actually. Not that it matters, we were planning to get caught in order to get close enough to help."

"What kind of plan is that?" Checks laughed. "I can get you close in, so's you can make a better 'un."

"Right," Wynd said. "Like we're supposed—"

"Is he dead?" Gage's question cut her off.

"Naw, just stunned." Checks turned over the smuggler and yanked off the man's frayed bit of rope belt. "Best to tie 'im up, so's he can't come after us."

Chapter Forty-Five
Mission Accomplished

"Shhhhh." Checks ducked low behind a row of jagged boulders and they followed. They raised their heads up just high enough to peer over the top of the rocks. There, at the very center of the pit, in the midst of a cloud of heavy dust, over a dozen streeters bent with long wooden rakes. Some scraped back the powdery ash while others sifted through it for small chunks of glittering rock. Their hands were wrapped in damp rags that steamed and sizzled when they handled the rocks. After setting the gathered ore into a barrel, they dipped their rag-covered hands into a bucket of murky water and sifted again through the piles of ash the others dragged away from the steaming vents.

Their faces were covered with whatever ragged bits of cloth they'd scrounged, sleeves torn from their own shirts or strips ripped from their trousers. Bony arms and legs were red and blistered. They coughed through their flimsy face coverings and toiled under the watchful eye of their kidnappers.

Off to the sides, a dozen men wearing fully functioning breathers and protective goggles kept their distance from the thick dust that churned around the streeters. Beyond them, their Captain sat in a tall-backed chair, a near twin to his shipboard seat. His right-hand man, Shields, fanned the swirling dust away from him as he ate sweets from a silver tray.

Checks ducked down and they sank to the ground beside him. "Welp, now's the ripe time for putting your capital plan into action, hain't it, Gage?"

"There're so many streeters," Wynd whispered. She'd tried to pick out her brothers from the others, but they were all covered in soot, their faces wrapped in rags. It was impossible to tell one streeter from another, Lostun' from Dartling, and who knew what other gangs. Here in this place, they all looked alike. Discarded kids forced into dangerous labor for the benefit of crooked adults.

"And so many guards." Gage shook his head, his brow wrinkled in worry. "Don't know how we can get everyone away and up that slanty hill."

Clax buzzed red on Gage's shoulder.

"But I thought you had a first-rate plan all worked out." Checks gave him a wide-eyed look of surprise.

Gage's shoulders slumped. "Yeah, well..."

"Admit it, Gage. You just don't have what it takes to lead." Checks shrugged, stood up and dusted himself off.

Gage grabbed at his shirtsleeve to yank him back down, but Checks brushed him off, pushing him off balance. Clax leaped from Gage's shoulder into the air, pulling out its sword in a flash of motion, but Checks whipped a length of heavy cloth from his back pocket and threw it over the clockwork. Clax struggled, slashing small gashes in the cloth, but

Checks bundled and wrapped it in more layers till it was caught tight. "Made a decent enough mask, but this is a much better use. Asides, I won't be needing rotted filter cloths and breathers much longer."

Wynd threw herself at Checks. Gage struggled to his feet and scrabbled to help Clax, but they found themselves suddenly surrounded by a gang of smugglers all wielding sharp blades.

"Ah," the Captain called out. "I see you've successfully tracked your quarry. Well done, Mr. Checks."

They stopped struggling.

"I knew it." Wynd glared at Checks. "Liar once is a liar twice."

Checks tossed the wadded fabric holding Clax into the air and caught it. A wide grin spread across his face. "Oh, Gage, you were always the most gullible-ist of all. A believer till the end."

Gage hung his head.

Chapter Forty-Six
Inside Job

The smugglers herded them over to where the Captain sat. The ragged streeters had stopped work and stared in their direction. A couple of the streeters tried to run toward them, chains rattling, but were forced back to the hissing vents and put back to work. "Get on with it," Shields hollered. "We've a schedule to keep."

Gage and Wynd stood in front of the Captain. He smiled, showing his teeth. "Well, we meet again." He tapped the tips of his fingers together, pleased with himself. "And how did you enjoy my little surprise?" He waved a hand at Checks. "Though, to be honest, it was all his idea. Clever and ruthless. Just my kind of crew."

Checks grinned and stepped forward. "I got you another present, Cap'n." He held out the wad of fabric with Clax inside.

"For me?" The Captain eyed the ball of dirty cloth, his upper lip curled. "Dear me, you shouldn't have."

"I think you'll like it." Checks thrust it toward him.

"Shields." The Captain snapped his fingers.

Shields stepped forward and grabbed the bundle. Clax buzzed inside and he nearly dropped it.

"Careful there. I wouldn't just let it loose," Checks told him. "Have you got something that might hold it?"

Shields eyed him. "It?"

"Yah. It's about the size of a small bird. So, a box or—"

"Just the thing." The Captain twirled a finger. "Shields. The cage."

"Cage, Cap'n?"

"Yes, yes. That canary we brought along to test the air." He extended a finger. "Well, the air here is terrible, what with all the dusty shards, so..." He shrugged and held out his hands. "But the cage might still be useful, eh?"

"Aye, Cap'n." Shields hustled off to a stack of crates and boxes. He searched through the pile till he found an empty wire birdcage and held it up in triumph.

"That'll work," Checks called.

Shields opened the cage door and shook the bundle of fabric out into it, slamming the door shut as Clax launched itself out of the tattered rags. The clockwork fairy crashed against the sides of the cage, buzzing and clanging, red sparks flying.

"Ah, ah, ah." Shields dangled the cage at arm's length to keep away from the point of Clax's sword. "Wouldn't be making sparks like that, was I you. The ore here about and the dust"—he waved a hand in the air—"is all quite volatile." He made an explosive gesture with his empty hand before he carried the cage back to the Captain,

Clax froze. Sword still drawn, the fairy gripped a

bar of the cage with one hand and chimed a question at Gage.

"Sorry, Clax." Gage's head hung lower. "So sorry."

"Very pretty," the Captain drawled. "I can't wait to take it apart and see how it works."

Clax jangled.

"No!" Gage shouted, his head snapping up. "You can't!"

"Oh, I can and I will. Well, not I, but one of my more skilled associates." The Captain leaned forward. "As for you, I have other plans."

Chapter Forty-Seven
The Honest Truth

"Welp, Gage, you done it again." Checks stood gloating beside him at the edge of a wide ditch. One end of it was closed off by a heavy metal gate. The other ended tapered to a narrow point.

Gage struggled against the ropes that bound him to a stack of crates at the edge of the pit.

"Cap'n's got a fine surprise in store for you, boy." Shields tightened the bindings that held Gage in place. "Cap'n's going to make use of that metal beastie what keeps tracking him hither and thither." Shields glanced across the ditch to where the Captain sat stiff-backed in his tall chair, his long fingers tapping a nervous rhythm on the arm rests.

Below them, the mechanical croc thrashed and roared in the ditch, snapping its jaws shut with a clang and clawing at the sides of the pit. Each time it threw itself at the sides and attempted to crawl out, one of the sailors standing along the edge shoved it back with a heavy boat hook.

"Don't rightly know as why it's taken a hankering to him that way." Shields tugged at the ropes to make sure they were secure. "Be that as it may. Comes in handy now and then. Been a right fine bogeyman for keeping those little buggers working the ore."

"What a fine mess you've made of it. Just like when you brung the law down on your poor old mam, eh?" Checks shook his head and stuck out his lower lip in an exaggerated pout.

"You leave my mum out of it." Gage clenched his fists. The day his mum had been taken to the workhouse, she'd already been ill for weeks. Her old breather had given out during a bad time. The smoggy air had got into her lungs. He'd stolen the peach in hopes the fruit would help her get better. But the coppers had caught up with him just outside the door to their tiny room. He'd been too quick for them, dodging and ducking and dashing away. But his mum had opened the door to see what the ruckus was and had called out to him to run. So, they'd nabbed her instead. Accusing her of being responsible for his theft. By the time he'd circled back home, the tender peach was ruined, bruised and leaking, and his mother was gone.

She'd been sentenced to a month in the workhouse. On the day of her release, Gage had waited all day for her to come out. That night, he finally got the nerve to ask after her.

"That'un—" The old man at the door sniffed at him. "Oh, she gone and expired afore her term were even half up."

Gage gritted his teeth against the memory.

"That's right. Bit of a sore spot for ya." Checks shrugged. "Too bad, though." He pointed at the end of the pit where Wynd stared over at them, two burly smugglers gripping her by the arms. "You just keep draggin' other people into yer troubles."

Across the ditch, the Captain waggled his fingers at Gage. On a table beside him, Clax clutched the bars of its cage. Flashing red and jangling so loudly, Gage could hear the sound from across the way. Though he couldn't make out everything Clax was saying, aside from a bit of angry cursing, the part he understood made his heart clobber inside his chest.

He shook his head.

"Looks like the show's about to start," Checks said. "'Bout time that dirty Dartling got what's coming to her."

The Captain held out his hand and gave a thumbs down. The smugglers holding Wynd, picked her up and dropped her into the pit.

Wynd landed with a thud.

The croc turned her way.

"Wynd!" Gage struggled against the ropes that held him tight.

"Gage. You have to keep your promise," she shouted at him.

"What?"

"You have to save them." She glanced up at Gage and shook her head. "Micah and Jasp. They aren't just mates. They're my brothers. My real brothers!"

The croc roared and gnashed its steely teeth and lunged at her.

Chapter Forty-Eight
Belly of the Beast

Wynd spun to face the croc as it bore down on her. "Not going down without a fight." She reached behind her and pulled out her sturdy pointy stick.

"Oh, goody." The Captain pulled his feet in and gripped the arms of his chair, staring at the pit with a mixture of fear and fascination.

The mechanical monster snapped its jaws, but Wynd dodged. She stabbed at it, but her stick just slid across the hard metal scales.

The croc spun around and swept her feet from under her with its tail. She fell to the ground. It twisted and snapped, but she rolled away, and all it caught in its teeth was air.

Wynd was breathing hard. She wouldn't be able to keep this up for long. And the metal croc didn't even need to breathe. Its energy source seemed endless.

Clax jangled wildly.

Energy.

Gage gulped and stared down at the ditch. He

knew what the clockwork was telling him. Knew what needed doing. If he could just reach his pocket. If he could get the sparker out and set it off. He looked across the way at Clax. Too close. It was too close. "Clax. I can't."

Checks stared open-mouthed at the sight below them, an ugly sneer on his face. It was a look Gage had seen plenty of times on adults like Cutter and Tinker. A look of savoring. A look of pleasure at someone else's pain.

It made him sick. He wanted to wipe that look off Checks's face. And more than that, he wanted to save Wynd and rescue their mates, and her brothers. To put what family they had back together.

The croc roared. Clax clanged louder.

The Captain clapped his hands together. "Goodness, this is exciting, isn't it Shields?" he called over the din.

"Aye Cap'n." Shields answered.

Gage tried to swallow down the emotions that churned his ding-danged innerds, but his mouth had gone dry. He struggled and wriggled, inching his hip closer to the side where he could almost reach.

The croc lunged again.

Wynd leaped aside.

Gage managed to get the tips of his fingers inside his pocket, sliding the sparker out.

Jaws opened wide.

Wynd shoved the pointy stick into the croc's mouth, jamming it up against the hinged section, wedging it open.

The croc roared from deep inside, gears grinding, pistons clacking. It thrashed its head wildly from side to side trying to loosen the stick.

Wynd backed away, hope fluttering across her face.

Gage fumbled the sparker. It fell onto the ground

beside him.

The stick snapped in two and the croc roared.

Checks stomped his feet and leaned forward over the edge of the pit.

Gage gazed down into the pit. "Sorry, Clax!" he shouted. "So sorry!"

Clax jingled and turned blue.

Gage pulled back his foot and kicked the sparker hard. It flew out over the croc and landed hard against the far wall of the ditch.

Snap! A bright spark flared.

The glow of the croc's eyes went dark. It fell to the ground with a screech and clatter.

Across the way, Clax collapsed onto the floor of the cage, and Gage's chest went hollow.

The Captain leaned forward in his chair with a startled look of horror and relief on his face.

Another spark lit up the side of the ditch. And another.

Then the ground shook. The volcano rumbled.

The Captain leaped up and backed away. His head swiveled to and fro. "What have you done?" he screamed. "Shields? Shields! Do something!"

The pit shifted and cracked open. Rocks tumbled and slid down the sides.

Shields grabbed the Captain by the arm and pulled him away from the widening ditch.

The ship's crew stumbled, scrambling away from spurting plumes of steam.

Checks fell onto his backside and crab-crawled away from the widening maw.

"Wynd!" Gage shouted. The crate he was tied to rocked on the edge of the pit. He struggled at the ropes holding him.

"I'm here." Using the croc's carcass as a stepper, Wynd pulled herself up the side of the pit and crawled out.

"I had to..." he bit his lips to keep from blubbering. "Clax wanted me to..."

"I know. I heard. I'm sorry." The ground shook again. She flicked her eyes across the pit to where Clax's cage teetered on the table. "Where's that knife of yours?"

Gage jutted his chin at his jacket pocket.

Smugglers hightailed away, as fast as they could stumble, leaving behind everything.

Wynd sawed at the bindings, cutting him free. "We have to get out of here."

"You help the others," Gage said, pulling off the ropes. "I can't leave Clax."

Wynd glanced across the widening crevice and shook her head. "Clax is gone, Gage. You can't help."

"Clax was family," he insisted. "We don't leave family behind. But you need to help your...your brothers and the Lostuns and...and the rest of the streeters." He choked out the words. "We made a promise."

"All right. I'll get the others out." Wynd nodded. "We'll meet you at the rim." She handed him back his knife. "And, Gage, be careful."

He gave her the gang nod. She hesitated a moment before returning it. Then she turned and rushed to help the streeters and hopefully find her brothers.

Chapter Forty-Nine
Nowhere to Run

The ground continued to shake. Gage ran to the end of the pit where the ground had not yet given way and leaped across the fresh cracks. He landed on the far edge and teetered a moment before shifting his weight forward and falling to his knees.

The wire cage had tumbled off the table, a lifeless Clax still inside. It lay on the ashy ground, less than a few dozen steps away. Gage pushed himself up, ignoring his bruised knees and bloodied hands, and rushed across the shaky ground. The island stopped shaking and went eerily quiet as he kneeled beside the cage. Tears dripped from his eyes. He wrenched open the door and reached in to pluck out his friend. He twisted the tiny key in Clax's back, knowing the gesture was worthless. The little clockwork lay still in his hand. He stroked the fairy's face with a fingertip. "I'm sorry, Clax." His grief let loose as he cradled the small clockwork to him.

The ground grumbled. A grinding sound drew his

eyes to the ditch and he watched as the croc's heavy metal body slid down the side and into the deep blackness that had opened below it. New vents split the ground around him, spewing steam and ash.

He wiped his face and gently slipped Clax into his pocket. There would be time to grieve later. Right now, he needed get out of there. He had to catch up with Wynd and the streeters and they needed to get somewhere safe.

He stumble-ran toward the end of the ripped open pit, but every time he thought he might be able to jump across, it widened just far enough to keep him trapped. He wasn't going to make it across. He'd have to find another way up. The smugglers had all disappeared from view, rushing toward the path he and Wynd and Checks had followed down into the crater. But the Captain and Shields had escaped from this side of the ditch. There must be another way out.

The air filled with steam and ash. He covered his face with the tail of his shirt as he scanned the black rocks. He suddenly felt as alone as he'd been on the streets after losing Mum. He wished Wynd was with him now to help. Might as well wish for Clax to still be alive, he thought. He had to make a choice, but he stood frozen in place. If he chose wrong, he could be trapped in a dead end. But if he stood there much longer, he'd choke on the sooty air. Or be steamed to death.

Another fissure erupted beside him. He picked a direction and ran.

Chapter Fifty
Out of the Fire

Wynd rushed across the rough ground, dodging the spewing plumes of steam that shot up hither and thither. Through the haze, she could make out the figures of the streeters. They were struggling to move across the shifting ground still chained together in groups of twos and threes.

"Micah! Jasp!" she shouted over the rumbling volcano.

A trio of streeters stopped, yanked still by the two boys on the end. "Wynd?" the tallest boy called out.

"Wynd!" shouted the shorter one. "Wynd!" He reached his arms out toward her and she fell to her knees and scooped him up. "Oh, Micah." She hugged him to her, and Jasp wrapped his long arms around both of them.

"Come on," yelled the other streeter. "We needs ta move."

Wynd shook herself free of her brothers, grabbed Micah by the hand and together, they rattled their way up the side of the slope and climbed out of the crater.

They collapsed on the ground in a heap, panting and coughing. For a moment, the mountain had quieted and an odd silence surrounded them.

"It'll start again any moment," Jasp told them, casting a nervous glance down into the crater. "And the dust is rising. We have to keep moving."

The streeters groaned, but one by one, Wynd urged them to their feet.

"We'd move a lot quicker without these ding-blasted chains," one of them grumbled.

A sudden whirring sound broke the silence. "I think I can help with that." Lufter dropped out of the sky, startling everyone but Wynd.

"Lufter!" she shouted. "You're late."

"Sorry." He settled his flyer and unbuckled himself from the harness. Then dug around in the tool box attached to the machine. "Didn't get the signal we were expecting."

Wynd looked down at the ground. "Yeah. Clax..."

"Let's leave it for later, shall we?" Lufter was already using his tools to set the streeters free of their chains. The island shook and growled. "Right now, we best get everyone down to the beach."

Chapter Fifty-One
All or Nothing

Gage stumbled across the bottom of the crater into a maze of rocks that confused and confounded him. More than once, he found himself facing a wall of rock.

He ran forward, then doubled back, till his anger boiled over. *Ding-dangity-blast it all! There had to be a way out.* But after another series of turns, he realized he was lost.

He considered turning around and trying to find his way back to the trench, but the ground shook and smoke roiled, sending him scurrying farther into the maze.

Round another bend, he stopped at a three-way fork. *Nothing for it, but to choose one,* he told himself. But he just couldn't make up his mind. He leaned against the rock wall to catch his breath and caught sight of an odd bit of fluff stuck to the rocks on his right. Was that? Feathers! 'Course the smugglers knew the way out. He ran down the right hand path and found another floofy bit. And then another.

He followed the tufts of the Captain's lost feathers through the narrow twists and turns till he came upon a rough stone staircase that had been hacked into the side of the crater.

Gage climbed the stairs on hands and knees to keep from being tossed off each time the volcano growled its anger into the world. There was no sign of the Captain nor his sniveling henchman, Shields, but he kept a watchful eye out, just in case. Near the top of the stairs, he turned and looked down. There was nothing to see except the dark vapor filling the bowl of the crater. Glittering dust clouded and swirled, mixing and rising toward him. Worse than Landings on its smoggiest day. The kind of bad air that would grate his throat and lungs and choke him through the flimsy filter mask he'd made of his shirt.

He put on a fresh burst to escape the rising threat and hauled himself the last few steps. He stumbled over the edge and fell smack into a panting Checks.

"Oy, Gage. What are you doing here? Why amn't you with your mates you was all in such a fuss to rescue?" Checks narrowed his eyes. "You've got a way off this blighted island, hain't ya?"

Gage glared at him. "If I had, I wouldn't tell you."

Checks grinned. "Welp, you're stuck with me now, either way. So might as well lead on." He shrugged. "Or we can stand here and get cooked like a couple o' meat pies."

Gage gritted his teeth. Part of him longed to do just that. He'd been no help to anyone. Not his mum, not his mates. Sure as not Clax. He had helped Wynd, but the cost had hurt. He laid his hand on his pocket where Clax lay tucked.

Checks caught the movement. "You got that baubledy-thing in your pocket, hain't ya?" He took a step toward Gage, reaching out a meaty paw.

Gage stepped back, his heels hovering over the edge of the stone stairway.

"Give it me."

"No," Gage said.

"What? The ragger-muffin's got his voice, now? Hain't that grand? How's about a trade, then?" He reached into his pocket and pulled out something round. Something that glinted in his hand. "It don't seem to tell time too good." He stared at the watch. Gage's watch.

"Where'd you get that?" Gage reached for the watch, but Checks snatched it away and held it out of reach.

"Found it, didn't I?"

"It's mine. Hand it over." Gage lunged for the watch.

Checks put a hand on Gage's head and held him back, keeping the watch well out of reach. "Come on then. Give me the shiny poppet, and you can have yer fancy bit."

The island rumbled.

"Quick now, afore we gets shook off the island."

Gage stepped back. Black clouds billowed up from the crater. His eyes burned, but not from the smoke. He wanted that watch. He'd guarded and hidden it all this time. Never able to let it go, even when the worst times had come. But now...he couldn't do that to Clax. His stomach churned like the billowing smoke. "No." The word came out choked.

"No?"

"No!" He ground his teeth and tried to step past Checks.

"Fine. Wasn't really gonna trade ya, anyhow." Checks grabbed Gage's jacket, yanking him off balance.

Gage stumbled forward. His pocket ripped open, spilling Clax onto the ground.

Gage lunged forward to grab Clax, curling around the tiny fairy like a protective shield.

Checks hauled back and gave Gage a hard kick. "Aw, look there, just like old times." He kicked him again. And again.

"Lay off!" Gage shouted.

"An' who's gonna make me?" Checks kicked again.

Tears leaked from Gage's eyes. He had lost his father's watch and now he was going to fail Clax. Again. The fairy had wanted a way out. Not to be owned. Clax deserved that. Even if it was only a clean quiet place to lay to rest.

No. He wasn't going to fail. Not again. With a rush of fury, Gage pushed to his feet.

"Do as yer good at and stay down!" Checks hollered.

Clutching Clax in one hand, Gage swung with the other, connecting with Checks's shoulder.

Caught in the midst of another kick, Checks stumbled to the side, then caught his balance. "You're goin' ta pay for that." He balled up his fists and rushed at Gage, swinging hard.

Gage ducked.

Checks's swing went over Gage's head. With a yelp, Checks fell forward. He tumbled over the edge and down the stairs, disappearing into the choking smog.

Gage crept to the edge of the crater. "Checks?"

No answer.

What had he done?

He stared down into the smoky haze.

Then he looked down at Clax. No. Gage wasn't to blame. Not this time.

Checks had caused this himself.

The volcano rumbled as if in agreement.

Gage ran.

***

Wynd and the streeters were a raggedy lot as they trailed down the outside of the crater. Lufter whirred in the sky above in his flying machine, scouting the way ahead and guiding them through the densest growth.

"Never thought I'd say it, but there's too much green stuff." Jasp hacked at the lush ferns and vines in front of them with the long-bladed knife Lufter had given him.

Wynd couldn't help but agree, and she wanted to laugh at the absurdity of it. She clung to Micah's hand, hope and joy and fear trading blows inside her head and heart. She'd found them. Finally. They were alive and together again.

The island rumbled and shook, causing her to stagger and reminding her they were not yet safe. Not till they were off this island and far from the street-nabbing smugglers. Them and their rotted Captain.

She glanced back to count heads and make sure everyone was still keeping up. She needn't worry. At the back of the line, Nobs, a full head taller than the rest, urged the others forward, keeping them moving.

She turned back just in time to keep from running into Jasp. He'd stopped of a sudden and stepped backward. "What is it?"

He put a finger to his lips and signaled for the streeters behind them to stop. Then he waved Wynd forward. She let go Micah's hand and stepped up beside him. They'd reached the edge of the jungle. The last of the dense greenery shielded them from the sloping beach where Gran stood supervising a small group of people, some of them ragged-looking kids, likely the other rescued streeters. They had dragged two small rafts down the sandy shore, leaving a pair of slithery trails in their wake. They'd stopped beside a group of small boats beached upon the shore, and were moving their stores from the rafts into the sturdier boats.

Wynd started to step out of the jungle, but Jasp grabbed her by the arm and pointed up the beach.

She bit her tongue when she spotted them.

The Captain trudged through the shifting sand, feathery hat akilter. His henchman, Shields, stumbled beside him, acting as a crutch to keep the Captain from falling over in his fancy shoes.

Behind them, a straggling line of smugglers slogged toward the small boats they had left pulled up on the shore.

The Captain halted, panting, and shoved Shields forward, pointing at Gran and her group of escapees.

"Oy!" Shields drew his sword and lunged forward. "You had best halt and desist!" He waved his blade through the air.

"Orders," the Captain shouted. "Orders, Shields."

Shields turned back and the Captain shook his head, jerked a thumb over his shoulder at the straggling gaggle of smugglers. Then, he pointed at the small group rushing to finish loading the boats and shove off.

"Oh, right. You maggoty blubberers heave to and stop them from stealing our boats!" Shields yelled over the rumble of the island's volcano.

Pulling out their weapons and kicking up a wake of gritty sand, the smugglers stumble-ran across the beach toward Gran and the others.

***

Gage stumbled, fell, picked himself up, and ran again. The island would shake, then still, then shake again. Like a steamer engine with a broken valve. It was just a matter of time before the pressure of all that steam and heat would burst loose. But Gage had no idea where he was heading or where Wynd and the rest of the streeters had got to. All he could think to do was run back toward the cliff where Quill and Lufter had set them down. With all the smoke and steam in the air, it was the only landmark he could make out. But what he would do once he reached it, he had no idea. There were no stairs up to the hangar that he'd seen. No way up on this side of the cliff.

As he steered his way down the slope, pushing though green brush and dodging around swaying trees, a shadow passed over him. He ducked and flattened out into the tall grass, then glanced up.

"Hey," Quill shouted down at him. "You look like you could use a lift."

***

Whooping and hollering, Wynd and Jasp and the rest of the streeters charged from the trees just as the smugglers drew near. They dragged long ropy vines from the underbrush, running circles around the men, tangling their legs and feet so they fell in clumps.

Lufter swooped down from above, harrying the men who managed to steer clear of the vines. He chased one then the other into the foamy waves where they disappeared from view, as if their legs had been pulled out from under them. They came up coughing and spitting and screeching to the sky, yelling of sea monsters and crawling back to shore where the streeters rushed them and wrapped them tight in thick, sturdy vines.

Shields plodded across the beach, huffing and puffing and hacking at the air with his wicked blade.

"Now!" Wynd shouted. Jasp hotfooted across the beach, swinging a set of manacles on their chain. With a yelp, he fell onto his face, rolled over and watched wide-eyed as Shields picked up speed and came at him. At that moment, Wynd drove in, slinging coconuts into the man's path. He stumbled and dodged, trying to keep his balance, but Jasp was already up and slipped behind him. Together, Wynd and Jasp pulled a daring Dartling shove-and-go. Shields went down, his sword whipped through the air tumbling over and over. It landed point down in the sand, the hilt vibrating from side to side.

"No!" he yelled, struggling to right himself as Jasp dove past him, grabbed the sword and thrust the point skyward with a whoop.

In moments, the entire crew of smugglers lay on the shore, groaning and covered in vines. Shields kneeled in the sand, looking lost.

Down the beach, the Captain took off his hat and threw it to the ground. The last of his ragged plumes drifted across the sand, while Gran and the streeters scrambled onto the smugglers' sturdy boats and pushed off into the waves.

***

Gage and Quill reached the island inlet and flew over a big rock. Out on the water small boats bobbed, dragging a couple of flimsy rafts behind them.

Wynd waved at him from the nearest boat. "Gage!"

"Wynd?" he called. "Did everyone make it out?"

She nodded. "But we still have work to do." She pointed ahead of them to where the smugglers' ship sat at anchor.

"Here," Quill said, handing him a heavy sack full of sparkers. "We have a boat to catch."

They flew across the water and buzzed the ship.

Lufter hovered high in the air, a tall boy hanging from the passenger harness of his flyer. "Look at me!" the boy shouted as Lufter dove down toward the ship. "I can fly!" He threw one sparker after the other onto the deck.

Caught off guard, the smugglers still on board rushed about in a confused frenzy.

Gage threw his own sparkers, aiming for the men's feet. Together, they herded the men toward the aft end of the ship. The four of them huddled there, unsure what to do, as sparkers exploded at their feet. Finally, one of them took off his dingy shirt and waved it in the air over his head. "Parley," he yelled. "We wants a parley."

"Hahahahaha," Lufter laughed. "What *we* want is you off this ship."

The men stared at him in disbelief. "Cap'n'll have our hides," one of them said. The other men nodded.

"Fine, then," Gage shouted. "I guess we'll just have to use the firebombs, then."

"But—" Quill started and Gage elbowed her. "Hang on while I dig out the anti-personable ones."

The men stared up at them, their eyes filling with fear.

"Right," Quill said loudly. "If we can't have the ship, then no one can. Back off, Luff," she called. "The flames are going to be huge."

Lufter grinned and flew his copter high above the ship.

"Woohoo!" the tall boy yelled as they ascended into the sky.

Gage grabbed the metal ball in his fist and pulled back his arm to throw. The smugglers huddled against the rail.

Gage heaved the sparker. It landed on the deck with a loud bang. The men leaped from the ship and into the water.

One of them screamed and all of them swam for shore, the sparkling fins of sea-kelpies cutting the water behind them.

Gage stared down after them. "Oy. I didn't expect to see them."

"Oh," Quill said. "Your clockwork bug was right. We made a deal."

"Clax"—Gage touched his pocket—"My *friend*'s name was Clax."

Chapter Fifty-Two
Finders Keepers

Gage stood on the deck of the ship. Across the water, the crater belched smoke and ash, the jade-green island disappearing behind a thickening darkness.

At the edge of the water, he could just make out the figures of the Captain and his henchman standing on the shore. What was left of the Captain's feathery finery flapped in the smoky breeze. Beside him, Shields slapped himself, again and again.

The rest of the smugglers, along with their dripping comrades, who had finally made it to the island, stared across the water at the ship.

"Gran still has a few tricks left in her." Lufter twirled a heavy wrench. "Grabbing their boats was an act of genius!"

"Put that away," Quill told him. "Before you hurt yourself." She handed Gage a copper spyglass. "Thought you'd like a better look." She pointed back at the island.

Gage put the spyglass to his eye, turning the ocular to bring the distant scene into view, and scanned across the greenery. A movement caught his eye and he swung back and narrowed the focus. A bedraggled figure limped toward the beach. Checks. So, he'd made it out, after all. Gage felt a wisp of relief mixed with the anger that still coiled inside him at his pack leader's betrayal.

Quill and Lufter's flyers rested strapped to the after deck. Gran stood at the helm, showing Nobs how to steer the ship.

They were headed for a distant island. One Gran said was as green as the one they were leaving behind and as much their home now as anyone's.

Wynd and Gage and the rest of the streeters had huddled up and agreed to form a new pack. Though, they still hadn't agreed on a name. Wynd was dead set on Starlighters, on account of Gran telling them they'd find their new home steering by the stars. But Gage wanted to honor Clax. Only, Tick-Tocks did seem a bit odd, and Clappers was straight out.

Sea water swirled and splashed behind them, a group of glittering fins cutting through the ship's wake. The sea-kelpies had helped them, after all. And now, they too, would have a new home.

"Hey, look what I found!" Lufter hoisted Hannigan's steam weapon into the air. "I wonder how it works." He plopped down cross-legged on the deck, his focus turned toward examining the weapon.

"Some things never change." Quill shook her head and smiled. "Sorry it took so long to get back to you," she told Gage. "But Gran…"

"Family. I know." Gage shrugged and gazed around the deck. His mates and the other rescued streeters stood at the rails staring out at the horizon. Lostuns, Dartlings and the rest, all shoulder to shoulder. Their faces wore a new expression. Gage stared at them, trying to place that look.

"Hope," Wynd said, suddenly beside him. "They have hope again. You gave them that." She held hands with a tall thin boy. The boy who'd been flying with Lufter. He'd found one of the Captain's fancy hats and had decided to wear it. A shorter, younger boy, who looked in need of a good scrub, clung to her other hand. Micah and Jasp. Wynd's brothers. She had found her actual family.

Gage's mood soured a moment, then he shook his head. He shouldn't be jealous of Wynd. After all, he had his mates, didn't he? Most of 'em anyways. The ones who were his real mates. *His* family. "Naw, we done it together."

Something poked him in the ribs. "Hey, now." He turned to glare at Wynd. "Thought you'd lost that ding-dang stick."

"What are you talking about?" Wynd gave him a side-eyed look.

Gage froze. Then scrambled to open up his jacket. He stared into his pocket. "Clax?"

A tiny jingle rang out.

"Clax!" He reached in and pulled out the clockwork fairy.

"Well, that's a surprise," Quill said.

Lufter looked up from the machine he was taking apart and blinked, wide-eyed. "I wouldn't have believed it, if I hadn't seen it."

They all stared while Clax flexed its fingers and inspected its limbs. The clockwork shook its head and gazed around in surprise.

"I can fix that wing," Lufter offered. "Maybe polish out those scuffs."

Clax, arms waving and wings abuzz, stood in a wide-footed stance, tiny fists on hips, and jangled loud and clear.

Gage laughed.

Lufter frowned. "What's so funny?"

"Clax says yes to the offer to fix its wing, but it'll keep the scuffs and scrapes, thank you. Says they add character."

"That's fair." Lufter grinned at Clax. "You earned 'em."

"Now, the whole family is here." Wynd smiled.

"Right." Gage lifted Clax up to perch on his shoulder and nodded. "The whole family."

Acknowledgements

Though writers mostly write alone, it takes a gang of people to turn the work into a book. My gang helped me patch the leaky steam tanks, check the valves, and ensure the completed product is worth a pence.

A ship full of thanks to my Beta Readers, Dawn V., Linda J., and Tanja B. for helping me to see where to add oil to the gears to keep them from grinding. Your honest and heart-filled feedback helped to make this story fire on all cylinders.

As always, to my fabulous editor, Anne Lind, who makes sure that every ding-dang word makes sense, this story just would not have been able to soar without you.

Bob Nelson, no one could ask for a more supportive (and patient) publisher.

Thank you, Keith Decesare, for envisioning and creating the amazing cover art. It's truly glorious and I am once more in awe of your artistic talent and your ability to take my vision and make it even better IRL.

Finally, I thank my lucky stars for all the readers who have shown my creative work an ocean of love over the years. I wish you all the best things always!

SHARON SKINNER grew up in a small town in northern California where she spent her time reading books, making up plays and choreographing her own musicals (when she wasn't busy climbing trees and playing baseball.) She's been writing stories since the fourth grade, filling page after page with fantastical creatures, aliens, monsters and, of course, heroes.

She is also an is an Author Accelerator Certified Book Coach and freelance editor, whose goal is to help writers weave their words into stories that shine.

Still a voracious and eclectic reader, Sharon also loves drawing, arts and crafts, sewing, and costume-making (especially steampunk). Her guiltiest pleasure is online gaming, and her biggest weakness is home-made, double-dark chocolate fudge. She lives in Arizona with her husband and three annoying but lovable cats.

You can find out more at
sharonskinner.com or bookcoachingbysharon.com